The Serpent

BOOK III OF THE FIRE TRILOGY

LISA VELDKAMP

DMP

The Serpent

BOOK III OF THE FIRE TRILOGY

LISA VELDKAMP

The Serpent

Cover Design by Rhianna Davies
Edited by Pam Elise Harris

ISBN 978-1-77400-024-3 print book
ISBN 978-1-77400-025-0 ebook

www.dragonmoonpress.com

Inquiries about additional permissions should be
directed to: lisa@the-elemental.co.uk

In loving memory of Torc, who first introduced me to druidry and who was not fortunate enough to have met an Eve to save him. Rest in peace, old friend…

The Serpent Whispers

I think it's *fair to say I made mistakes in my life. Some would even say I've done a lot of wrong. I'm sure I have. My intent has always been pure, though. It's not easy to be able to see the future and not intervene. For every change has its consequences. Sometimes the consequences are so great, they cause a ripple effect. Through time. And with it, the people involved. This is my burden to bear.*

It is ironic that I based my company on people with special abilities when I did everything in my power to give my granddaughter a normal life. A life away from the people who work for me. I guess we make exceptions for the ones we love. Double standards, my daughter would say, but she doesn't know I'm alive. No one does, but William and one other.

His name is Tristan Visconti, and he's in love with my granddaughter. Just like I knew he would be. He's my way back to her. For the time has come for Catherine to join the Company. A serpent can only shed its skin so many times and my final shed is approaching.

Her birthday is coming up, and with it, a present I preserved for her will be activated. It will show her a piece of the puzzle, which will lead her to me. At least, that's the plan. Sometimes, visions have a life of their own. Sometimes, I get it wrong.

Eve

I can't remember *being on the run before. Not from the people I've always considered my friends. Family even. I never had to run. People usually run away from me, and that has suited me just fine. So, this is unchartered territory for me. Which is kind of exciting. Also, kind of scary. Scary because I'm flying without the safety net of the Company I'm running from. The people who've always been there to protect me are now the people chasing me. Because they want me back. And not just me. They also want Alan, the man I ran away with.*

Eve turned to look at Alan, who was still blissfully asleep. She sighed. Several weeks had gone by now since the world had almost come to an end, and they were approaching the end of December. November had been unusually warm for the time of year, but after that the cold had crept back in again. With a vengeance, it seemed. Eve shivered and pulled the duvet a little higher up. She did not regret the decision to run away with Alan. She did regret leaving Tristan behind. She'd only received one encrypted message from him so far. The Company would give him hell for letting her and Alan go. Because they had ways to figure that out and they would have by now. A part of her longed to hear from him, to know he was okay. She knew he would have given them as much of a head start as possible, but so far, they'd had to relocate twice. Yesterday she had come eye to eye with Roy, Tristan's right hand and best friend. Alan and Eve had decided to split up, to throw them off and Roy had gone after her, while Tristan had chased after Alan. It was a logical choice, she knew that. Roy would have stood no chance against Alan since he was able to control anyone's mind. Tristan was an empath himself, though. Alan's powers would not work on him. Still, it bothered her. She would have given anything to read Tristan's mind for just a minute. Instead, she'd had to settle for Roy's thoughts. His mind had been practically screaming at her when they made eye contact.

The Serpent has full focus on you. Stay unpredictable, for God's sake! Oh, and are you okay?

She smiled. That had been kind of cute. She never would have thought there would be a day she and Roy would be friends again. Not after her break-up with Tristan. Saving an entire planet had apparently helped put things back into perspective, for all of them. She had given him an almost imperceptible nod to answer his question and had to duck a split second later to avoid the beam from the company's energy taser. Normally that would have pissed her off. Now she almost had to laugh at the memory. Roy's aim had been unfocussed and he'd missed her by more than an inch. Roy never missed. He'd let her go on purpose. Again. Just as Tristan had given up the chase on Alan. They would have to become more careful going forward, though. Eve had taken Roy's advice to heart and had made a split decision to jump into the B&B they were currently staying in. Eve never would have picked it, and that alone made it perfect. She was a hotel or an apartment kind of person. She hated to share and the cosiness of the place. It reminded her of her time with Tristan. Even though she didn't think of Tristan as a potential lover—not anymore, at least—she still didn't need the reminder of their time together. However, beggars could not be choosers, and it was a good hideout. Alan stretched and moved closer to her to put his arm around her.

"Good morning, gorgeous. Did you sleep well?" he mumbled, his eyes still closed.

Eve smiled. "For the first time in days, yes. Life on the run isn't as thrilling as they make it out in the movies, now is it?" She reached out to push back a lock of his long, white hair. He made a humming noise.

"Oh, I don't know. Life is pretty interesting from my perspective. Then again, I would find almost anything interesting, having been asleep for so long."

Eve knew Alan did have memories from his "slumber-period" as they were now calling it. She had actually been able to help him pick up on some thoughts she heard in his mind and through gentle interrogation, they'd retrieved quite a few memories together.

It seemed Alan had been able to choose how he spent his time in the mental hospital. Meaning, he could actually be at the mental hospital or visit the astral plane in his mind. Being a highly intelligent man, Alan had realized quite quickly he was able to leave his body behind and travel the world on the astral plane. Some people referred to it as an out-of-body experience, but Alan discovered it was so much more than that. As an empath, he could influence people's emotions. Their responses. This didn't work any differently on the astral plane. He learned how to penetrate peoples' dreams. First as an innocent bystander, but as time went by, he learned how to take control of their dreams as well.

Eve had been fascinated by his progress, and they'd shared information. She herself had been assigned to the Company's latest project—Dreamcatcher. Comatose people who for some reason didn't wake up. Many people died from their injuries, and then there were those who woke up after a couple of days or perhaps weeks. Some, however, did not wake up. Physically, they should have been able to wake up, but something was holding them back. Doctors could not explain this group of people. Which was why the Company had taken an interest. Anything unexplainable made their heads turn. Being their top mind reader and the only known reviver in the world, Eve had been the logical choice for this special project.

And she'd had some pretty interesting results before their abrupt escape. These people had also figured out how to leave their bodies behind. How to astral travel and create a life there. A better life. Or so they thought, at the very least. Eve had picked up on their every thought and these people were happy. Way too content to return to their bodies. They lacked incentive.

Alan had told her he'd experienced something likewise. Once his powers on the astral plane began to grow, he'd become more and more detached from his physical body, going back to the mental hospital less and less. Which was why his eyes had been so completely vacant the moment Eve had arrived at the hospital. He hadn't really been there.

Alan looked into her eyes. "What are you thinking?"

She didn't even hesitate in responding. "I was thinking about Dreamcatcher. I think the Serpent must have known we were very close to losing you forever. Good thing I was able to bring you back." She gave him a kiss, which he prolonged.

"I'm still having a hard time dealing with the fact your boss— excuse me—former boss, is Kate's grandmother."

Eve frowned. "I know. I thought I had met the Serpent one time, just before Dreamcatcher, actually. Turned out that was her blocker. One of the best. Couldn't get a damn thing from him." They'd received an encrypted message from Tristan containing this information with specific instructions that Catherine, or Kate as Alan called her, was not to be informed about this minor little detail until further notice. Should they run into each other. And they would. She was sure of that.

"Do you think I would have?" he asked.

She shook her head. "No. Blockers block out thoughts and emotions. Depending on their strength, they can also block other people in close proximity. The only thing you would have noticed is that you wouldn't feel anything coming from them. Emotions, I mean."

Alan had a thoughtful look on his face. "Then I probably ran into one or two. I always thought there were people like in *Twilight*, you know?" He looked at her. "Like Edward's Bella, so to speak."

"I didn't realise you read *Twilight*," Eve said.

"I haven't been in a coma all my life, you know, and I do know how to read. Even if it's *Twilight*," he said in a teasing voice.

Eve rolled her eyes. "Well, basically that's precisely what it is. In her human form, Bella can block out his mind-reading, and as a vampire, she can even protect others. So yes, that's basically the same. Makes you wonder where Stephanie Meyer got that particular idea, doesn't it?" she said with a smile, which he returned.

"Charles is a blocker, isn't he?"

Eve nodded. "The best I know, with perhaps the exception of the Serpent's blocker."

Her mind drifted. Charles. Charles had been working for the Company for as long as she could remember. He had guided both her and Tristan. Charles took people under his wing, he was a caretaker. At least, when you were in his good graces. She hadn't been lying when she'd told Tristan she missed him. She did miss Charles. They had spent so much time together, Her, Tristan, Roy and Charles. Whatever Charles had thought about her, she'd always liked him. Like an absent father. Her own parents had never been around, and Charles had looked out for her, even though she had given him a hard time. She had met Cherise, his stepdaughter, several times and had always felt quite envious of how much he loved her. Charles had always made her feel protected, though, loved even. For that, she would be forever grateful.

Alan picked up on her emotions, and she answered the question in his mind. "Yes, I'm glad we're on good terms again. There are few people who are important to me, and he was one of them. I'm glad he's in my life again. Charles and I used to be a pretty good team, you know."

Alan frowned.

"Oh, don't fret, my love. I didn't mean it like that. You know Tristan and I were an item. You don't hear me bitching about Catherine, do you?" She looked him straight in the eyes.

His face relaxed. "No. You don't. For which I'm grateful. I let her down. Probably in the worst way imaginable. One way or the other, I will find a way to restore that balance. And she has to know she's not a master of death anymore. Before she tries anything stupid. Not that she would. I think. No, Kate would never use her powers for her own personal gain."

When the asteroid was about to hit the Earth, Catherine had prevented it by using her powers both as an elemental and a master of death, having gained that last particular power during a face-off with Alan years ago at an industrial site that had sent him to the mental hospital, comatose. The blast from the asteroid had Catherine flying through the air, smashing her body into a tree with enough impact to stop her heart. Eve had been forewarned that this would happen by the Serpent. Or the person who she'd then thought to be the Serpent. Eve and Alan had rushed to the site, colliding with Tristan, Roy and Charles. Alan had knocked Roy and Charles out cold, much to Tristan's dismay. It had been the most logical choice at the time. They couldn't afford a lot of witnesses and it would give Roy and Charles plausible deniability, as Eve had explained to Alan. She had doubted whether Tristan would see it that way, but she had gone with her instincts. Eve had been able to revive Catherine, but in the seconds she had been officially brain-dead, Alan had felt his power return to him. Once revived, they stayed with him and didn't jump back to Catherine. Eve later said this made sense, as it had been his power to begin with.

"Well, I can't but agree with you on that particular aspect. She is as white as they come, as we would say at the Company. However, I'm sure Tristan will find a way to let her know."

Alan laughed. "You might see a different side to Kate once she finds out her grandmother is alive and kicking and actually head of the company her beloved Tristan is working for. Mind you, you did stress to him the importance of her finding out sooner rather than later, right? I know Kate. She hates betrayal. She's loyal to a fault, and she's going to have kittens over Tristan if she finds out he's known for months. I don't even want to know what she's going to do or say to her grandmother."

Eve shrugged. "Well, as far as the Serpent's concerned, I'm sure she already knows how…Kate…is going to react." She was still trying to get used to Alan's version of her name. "She is the greatest seer we've ever had, after all. As for Tristan, he can handle himself. Besides, she forgave him for lying about his involvement, right? She'll forgive him again."

He frowned. "I'm less sure about that, but you could be right. We should get up, my love, or we'll have to do without breakfast."

"Which is why I loathe these B&B's. I hope those Italians from yesterday have moved on. I swear, that woman wouldn't shut up." Eve shivered.

Alan laughed and got up from the bed. "We could always scare the living daylights out of them. That would make for an interesting morning." He grinned at her before moving towards the en-suite bathroom. Eve threw a towel in after him, which he neatly caught in one hand.

"Too slow, love."

* * *

"It is such a lovely county, isn't it? Could you pass me the sugar, dear?"

Eve reached for the sugar and put it in front of the older woman. Thankfully, the Italians had left. However, in their place, an older British couple had arrived. They were travelling the Lake District and decided upon Grasmere because of its beautiful scenery and cosiness, the cosiness Eve normally tried to avoid at all costs. Truth be told, she did like the older woman. There wasn't a rude or negative thought in her mind, but as often the case with social people, they took a great interest in Alan and herself. What did they do, how did they meet, had they seen anything worthwhile? Alan, being a former teacher, had a natural flair for explaining things, and Eve was grateful she only had to put in a word or two and hum or smile at the appropriate moments.

"No, it's easy distance. As I understood from our hostess, there is a nice little pub along the way to stop for refreshments. And you're in luck, for it looks like it's going to remain dry for the day."

"Yes. George checked this morning on the weather app, didn't you?" She gave Alan a smile, while patting her husband's hand. "I'm not much use with today's technology, but George took quite a fancy to the iPhone, and I'm glad he did. I have to admit, it can be very useful. I'll have you know we Stype for free to our daughter in New York. How about that!"

George tried to hide a smile. "Skype, Beatrice, it's called Skype."

"Oh right. Well, never mind. It is a great technique and all in such a little device. This is our last day here in Grasmere, you know. Tomorrow we're flying out to our daughter in the United States. George still owns the company, you see, and they have a private plane. It is such luxury, I tell you."

Alan gave her a dazzling smile. "That is absolutely wonderful, Mrs…"

"It's Fletcher, dear, but please call me Beatrice."

Alan gave a big sigh. "We've always longed to see New York, haven't we, my love?"

Eve immediately understood where he was going with this and nodded. "Yes. Central Park in winter is supposed to be really something. I even have an aunt there, but the flights are rather expensive, you know." She gave an apologetic smile to Mrs. Fletcher.

She could feel the persuasive vibes rolling off Alan and tried to keep a straight face. Mrs. Fletcher looked at her husband, who nodded his consent.

"Well, why don't you come with us? Do you have any time left? I'll tell you what. You get hold of your aunt and ask her if it would be convenient for you to come over and if so, you'll be our guests on the plane."

Alan gave them an embarrassed look. "Are you sure? I mean, we couldn't possibly accept. It's such a generous offer. You hardly know us."

Mrs. Fletcher waved his concerns away. "Nonsense, we'll have none of that! You're obviously good people, and I do so love the style of your lady, Alan," she said with a wink. "You remind me of a younger self, my dear." She looked at Eve.

Mr. Fletcher squeezed his wife's hand and gave her a loving smile. "Really, we'd love to. Two young people in love should be able to visit the Big Apple. Let us help in the small way we can."

Alan looked at Eve. "Then we gracefully accept and thank you in advance for your kindness. Darling, I think it's best you try to reach your aunt this afternoon. She'll be asleep right now, won't she?"

"Ah yes, the time difference. Well, that works out perfectly. We'll have an answer when you get back from your walk, Mr. and Mrs. Fletcher. I can't wait to tell her. She'll be so surprised." Eve made sure she sounded as excited as possible.

Such lovely people. I'm glad we can do something for them, Eve could hear in Mrs. Fletcher's mind.

"Oh please, dear. Beatrice and George. Really, I insist. After all, we'll be travelling companions soon. Shall we have tea together here at four? Would that be convenient for you both?"

Alan looked at Eve and confirmed. "That would be lovely… Beatrice," he said with a smile. They all stood to leave the breakfast room, thanking their hostess, who just walked in again to clean up. Eve and Alan quickly departed to their own room, still hearing the older couple talk to their hostess about their outing for the day.

"That was quick thinking, love. Good work." Eve sat down on the bed.

Alan kicked off his shoes and sat down on the comfy chair in the corner. "It's our first stroke of real luck. What are the odds? They have their own freaking plane! Well, your company has planes, but we can't really access those, now can we?" he said with a grin.

Eve laughed. "No. Well, not without some serious mind control. Even then, we'd have a tough time remaining undetected."

Alan became serious. "And you're sure New York is where we'll have to be?"

Eve nodded. "Yes, I'm absolutely sure. At least. I'm sure the Serpent is sure about that, if that makes any sense? Kate will leave for New York two days from now, right after her birthday. They're spending New Year's in Leah's apartment. Probably not all of them, but Kate and Deborah most likely will. I'll check with Roy when I get the chance. If memory serves correctly, her whole inner circle will be there. And Tristan did say Leah saw something horribly wrong with the ball drops. He'll need us there. The tricky part will be to aid Tristan and his team while staying out of other Company hands." She sighed.

"You're worried?" he asked.

She shrugged. "I don't know. I'm just on edge. It can hardly be any worse than the end of the world, right? And we survived that."

Alan gave her a soft smile. "But you don't like it."

It wasn't a question. She knew he could feel her anxiety. Eve shook her head. "I think it's just me in this case. Normally I would have all the knowledge of the Company at my disposal and now we're flying blind. I don't like it. It makes me nervous."

"You don't have to do this. You know that…," Alan started to say.

"I'm not turning you in. End of discussion, Alan. We talked about this before. I'm not doing it again."

He smiled at her. "Okay…I love you, too."

Eve's breath hitched. It was the first time he actually said he loved her. She stood up from the bed and sank down before the chair, taking his hands in hers. "And I you. Maybe there will come a time when I can go back to the Company, but I'm not doing it without you. As long as they're after us and the Serpent won't tell us the big picture, there's no point in going back. I'm tired of being in the dark, wondering if what I do really is for the greater good or not. Besides, I have to keep you on the right track and protect you poor tainted soul." She gave him a devilish smile.

Alan laughed. "Yes, my poor tainted soul. I think it's in desperate need of some genuine loving." And he carried her to the bed.

Catherine

Saving the world *and dying in the process does something to a person. It leaves a mark. It also takes away a piece of the puzzle. The puzzle that is me. In my case, the ability to control death. In all fairness, it was never mine to begin with, and I do hope it returned to its owner. He might be worthy of it now, and he's not alone. I am. For Tristan has left me. I know he had to. I know he loves me, but I still don't like it. I need him. To protect me from the nightmares. Always the same. I swear, it's watching me, waiting, biding its time. Only this time, there's no Alan hiding in the cornfield. It's something else. Someone else. I think it's a woman.*

Catherine awoke drenched in her own sweat. Someone was screaming. It took her a second to realize the scream was coming from her. She sighed and turned on the light on her nightstand. That was it. She'd had enough. She got out of bed and walked to the other side of the room. Nothing. The painting was completely empty, all she could see was corn. Lots of corn, in a luscious field. *The Sacred Valley of the Incas* stared back at her. It made her feel uncomfortable. She had first seen it in a dream. In the dream, the painting had sucked her inside. Seeing the same painting the next day while visiting the National Gallery with Leah had not exactly calmed her nerves. Worse even, Leah had been having visions of her getting sucked into the painting. A shiver ran down Catherine's spine.

"Alexa, turn on main light." The lights went on, and Catherine took a closer look. Still nothing. She sighed. "I'm officially starting to lose my mind."

She knew Alan had gone to a lot of trouble to get it into

her home. After some debate, her inner circle had decided the painting should remain with Catherine. She gave the painting another stern look.

"Well, that's all just peachy, but you're not staying here." She took the painting from the bedroom wall and walked downstairs towards the living room.

Catherine's home was located in Shoreditch, London, her favourite part of the city. The former industrial building now occupied several luxurious apartments, and Catherine was the proud owner of the penthouse, which came with a magnificent rooftop terrace to sit and relax or throw a nice party. She could enjoy it all seasons because she had an optional see-through glass ceiling installed, which she could open or close.

Her ground floor was divided into two spaces. Her own personal living space and that of her company Elements, which she now shared with Deborah, one of her best friends. Deborah became a full partner a couple of years ago. They were both qualified massage therapists. Combined with Deborah's healing and empathic powers and Catherine's elemental powers of earth, air, fire and water, they had become quite successful, especially among the rich and famous, who did not only leave their practice a lot more relaxed, but Elements had helped many of them overcome their addictions. Catherine was still very grateful that when she decided to move from the Netherlands to the UK to live closer to her mother, Deborah, who had lived near her in the Netherlands had simply just packed her things and asked when they would be leaving.

Catherine loved her home. It had an earthy vibe. Leah always referred to it as a modern version of a *Lord of the Rings* style. Catherine looked at the moss wall, which separated her personal space from their company.

Perhaps somewhere inside Elements? No, she wouldn't be able to check on it fast enough. Catherine sighed. The guest bedroom then where she put Tristan's cello for safekeeping. She lifted the painting and took it back up again to the largest guestroom. Making an effort to ignore Tristan's cello in the far-left corner, she took down a medium-sized painting off the wall by Magne Furuholmen and replaced it with the dreaded cornfield.

"Sorry, Mags. I'll find another spot for you." Catherine took a step back to admire her handy work. Better. Definitely better. This was three nights in a row now. Stupid painting. Somewhere on the same floor, she heard a buzzing noise. Bugger! Her phone. Who could be calling her in the middle of the night?

Catherine sprinted towards her own bedroom and picked up her iPhone. Leah. Of course, she should have known.

"Heya, girl. I'm okay, just another stupid nightmare."

"Goodness, Kate, this has got to stop. One of these days you're going to give me a heart attack," Leah said to her.

Catherine sighed. "I know. So sorry, hon. Just out of curiosity, what did you see?"

"Same old shit. You getting sucked into that blasted painting. I'm going to say it one more time, for the record, I was not in favour keeping that thing in your apartment."

Catherine smiled. "I know. You made that perfectly clear. However, you did not object when the group overruled you." She heard Lee make a tutting noise.

"I harrumphed, if you will remember."

Catherine let out a laugh. "Yes, I do remember. Oh, thanks, Lee. I needed that. Look, I don't like it, either. If I'm perfectly honest, that thing is giving me the creeps. You'll be glad to hear I moved it out of my bedroom into the guestroom."

"Oh, that is a vast improvement indeed."

"Sarcasm?" Catherine asked. She heard Leah laugh.

"Actually, no. You're losing your touch, Kate. That was genuine relief. I thought you were mad as a snake to keep it in your own bedroom anyways."

"It's three am in the freaking morning, Lee. Forgive me for not being my brightest, perky self, okay."

"More towards half four, if you want to be nitpicky. You probably woke up at three. Same as yesterday, right?"

Catherine sighed. "Yes. And the day before that. Starting to become old news. Maybe it'll be over by tonight."

"Because it's your birthday, you mean?" Leah asked.

"Yes. I actually had several scenarios. At first, I thought it might be connected to the midwinter solstice. You know, returning of the light and all that, but nothing happened. Then I even considered Christmas, though I'm not getting a Christian vibe of this painting, but who am I to judge?"

"And, yet again, nothing happened," Leah replied.

"Nope. Nothing. So, then I thought, maybe it's connected to my birthday? Thirty-six is a special number, after all." It remained silent on the other side of the phone. "Lee, are you still there?"

"Still here. I was mulling over what you just said. Hadn't really thought about that. I'm googling it as we speak. Here we are. The symbolism of number thirty-six is above all the principle of creativity. It is a creation of a number nine that gathers abilities of all previous numbers. It is also connected to the number three because it can be divided by nine three times. Number three, which symbolized the Trinity, signifies Heaven, Earth, and in between are angels." Leah sighed. "Sounds like a lot of mumbo jumbo to me, Kate."

Catherine laughed. "Don't tell Sue or Deb, they're quite fond of symbolism in numbers." She heard Leah sigh.

"I'm not saying it's total bullshit. I'm sure there's a lot to be said for numerology. It just sounds a bit far-fetched to me. That is all."

"As opposed to stopping an asteroid by using the elements and my borrowed powers as a master of death?" It remained silent for another few seconds.

"Excellent point. I'll shut up now." That made them both laugh.

"Okay, so let's both try and get some shut-eye for what's left of the night, otherwise we'll be useless by tonight," Catherine said, still laughing.

"Do you need any help preparing for your birthday party?" Leah asked.

"Nah. Not much to do, really. I've got everything I need, and I still have way too many rations from the asteroid shopping spree. Besides, it'll be more like a small gathering. No hootenanny."

"Not even a shindig?" Leah asked.

"Nope. Just lots of brie and mellow song stylings. Oz would not approve," Catherine laughed at her Buffy reference. It was still one of her favourite TV series that ever aired.

"A gathering it is. Comes with the age, darling. Nothing wrong with a good piece of brie."

Catherine gritted her teeth. "Thanks, love. I'll go and fetch my wheelchair now, okay?"

"You do that, honey. Love you!" And the line disconnected.

"Bitch," Catherine said but smiled as she put her phone back on her nightstand. Almost four. If she was lucky, she could get another five hours in. This was probably going to be a day where her coffee would need coffee.

Tristan

Keeping a secret *from the one you love does something to you. It slowly starts to nibble on the edges of your soul. She says it is pivotal to let this run its course. The Serpent, also known as Catherine's grandmother. It should all be over by the end of today. Catherine's birthday. I don't know if I can do this. I kept her in the dark once, and I made a vow to myself to never do that again. So, it all comes down to trust. Do I trust her? Does she have Catherine's best interest at heart? I have to believe that. She sacrificed her own life to protect that of her granddaughter. That has to count for something, right? I'm sick and tired of secrets, though. Time to come clean about something.*

"Boss, are you coming, or do you need another cup of coffee?" Roy looked at his best friend and boss, Tristan Visconti. They had been called in by the Company. In the middle of the night, but that was not out of the ordinary. Annoying, yes, but not out of the ordinary. Tristan looked tired, he thought. Not a good sign. They were working him too hard. And something had been bothering him. Something besides Catherine.

"No, I'm fine," Tristan replied. "On second thought, another cup wouldn't kill me. Mind you, these all-nighters might." He sighed.

"So, this is what? Third night in a row, now?" Roy asked while Tristan filled up his cup with a double espresso this time.

"Yes. Three time's a charm?" He pulled his mug from under the coffee machine and stretched out his hand to Roy. "Refill?" Roy gave him his mug.

"Sure, why not?"

They walked through the hallway towards Tristan's office. At this hour, the Company was eerily quiet and they listened to the sound of their own footsteps, which softly resonated on the marble beneath their feet. When they reached the corner, Tristan pressed four fingers on the screen on the wall and the dark, wooden door gave a click. He held it for Roy and closed the door behind them.

He pulled something out of a nearby drawer and swiped the room.

"Good. No new bugs. We're clear." In the aftermath of the asteroid event, Tristan and his team had had a hard time, since they had been accused of losing both their only reviver and top mind reader and, of course, Alan. Tristan cared very little, but he did not like being spied on by his own company. So, they'd made a habit of sweeping each room before having a serious conversation and even then, they sometimes chose to use a burner phone to send messages to one another.

Roy had installed himself behind one of the partner desk's in Tristan's office. "So, they are leaving early in the afternoon for New York?" he said, glancing at his laptop.

"Yes, Catherine, or more accurately, the girls, wanted to celebrate her birthday here in London, and then they're flying out to Leah's in New York. At least, Catherine and Deborah are staying at Leah's. I think the rest of the girls are staying in a nearby hotel."

Tristan swiped through his phone looking for something. "Yes, I have it right here. Reservation at the Wellington Hotel. Two double rooms and one single have been booked. Do we know if their partners are tagging along for this little outing? I'm pretty sure Sue's partner would be busy until well in the new year, right?" Tristan looked up from his phone to see Roy's response.

Roy shrugged. "I can check. To be honest, it wasn't high on my priority list, but it's a five-minute job to find out. You want to know?"

"Yes, please. I've learned that when Catherine's involved, it's best to know as much as possible." He heard Roy snort and gave him a look.

"Well, I'm just saying, boss. You're not wrong. Okay, I'm on it. Anything else you need?"

Tristan shrugged. "Besides the blasted painting, you mean? No, not really." He reached inside his pocket, pulled out a different phone and texted *Any other news?*

He saw Roy check his other phone as well but made a show of going about his own business. In the Company, they never knew who was looking over their shoulder, even with their precautions. After a few minutes, his phone vibrated.

They're fine. Still Lake District. All set to move to NY as well. Location unconfirmed. R

Tristan smiled and pocketed his phone when he heard a knock on the door and stood up to open it.

"Morning, lads. My, this place is like a graveyard at five in the morning. Took me ages to find a decent cup of coffee, but I finally managed. Thank you, sir." Charles said to Tristan who was holding the door for him when he entered the room holding up a tray with three steaming mugs on it.

"Where did you get these?" Roy said, picking up one mug. "Oh, just smell that!"

Tristan shook his head but gratefully picked up a mug as well. "Cheers, Charles. You do know we have a machine just at the end of the hallway, right?"

Charles just looked at him.

Tristan sighed. "Never mind."

Charles smiled. "Angie in the A-wing was kind enough to open the coffee corner for me. And you both have to admit, so much better than the mud that machine calls coffee."

"Poor Angie, but bless her heart, it does taste divine," Roy said, taking another sip. "I didn't even know our catering staff began this early."

"They don't," Charles replied. "They start at six for the early shift, but I know Angie's always early. Likes to prepare and take her time. Nice girl."

Tristan laughed. "To you everyone under forty is a nice girl,

Charles. Angie's well in her thirties. I think you can safely call her a woman."

"Well, she's still a spring chicken to me, sir. Speaking of which, the lights are out again, so I think Miss Catherine went back to sleep. I drove by her apartment on my way here."

"Thank you, Charles." Tristan gave him a soft smile.

After the asteroid incident, as Roy liked to call it, they had removed all the bugs and cameras from both Catherine's home apartment and Elements. They had considered leaving a tracer on the girls' phones, but Roy had said it was too risky. He was good, but so were their colleagues at the Company. Somebody else might find a way in as well and expose messages they did not want out in the open. Tristan had filled them in about being in contact with Eve, and through her, Alan. Also, that he'd left his cello with Catherine for safekeeping.

There was a downside, of course. He could no longer keep an eye on Catherine, which left him on edge. Yes, he'd left his cello in her possession. Catherine would know how to interpret that gesture. He trusted her with his most prized possession, but not being able to speak to Catherine or hold her in his arms for just one moment was starting to weigh him down. And he still wasn't sure exactly what was going to happen today. He'd seen plenty of things in his years at the Company to keep an open mind, but paintings coming to life was just a bit too much on the fringe side. Then again, stranger things had happened. All he could do was try to be there for Catherine to the best of his ability. He had no idea how she was going to react to the news her grandmother had been alive this whole time. Let alone the fact she was the CEO of the Company. Or her grandmother's plans for Catherine. Because there was one thing Tristan was absolutely sure of. The Serpent had plans for Catherine. Whether or not he was going to like those plans was yet to be decided. Fact was, he knew very little. At least with the asteroid, they had been in the loop. Except for maybe how things were supposed to play out. In all fairness, if he'd known Catherine would die during the asteroid attack, he would have probably intervened and things might have turned out quite disastrously.

There was that little word again. Trust. Who do you give it to, and who really deserves it?

"There is something I want to discuss with you. Something that has to stay within these four walls." Roy and Charles both stopped with their work and looked at him.

"Sounds serious, sir," Charles said.

Tristan nodded. "It is. It's about the night of the asteroid, the immediate aftermath, so to speak. I've been struggling with this the last couple of weeks, but in the end, I think it's better that you're in the loop."

Roy looked at him. "I didn't realise we'd been out of the loop, boss."

"A request from Eve. Before you start, for your own good, she thought it would be better if you and Charles didn't know, so you could at least have the safety of plausible deniability. And to some extent, it did work because neither of you got demoted." He ran a hand through his hair.

Charles gave him a speculative look. "They were there, weren't they? At the edge of the circle that night."

Tristan nodded.

"Ah bollocks, I knew it!" Roy cried out. He pulled out his wallet and handed a ten-pound note to Charles. "You were right, man."

"You knew?" Tristan asked.

Roy shrugged. "Not for sure, but both me and Charles suspected as much. I've never seen Trevor so upset. Then you got demoted to your original status, and we were stuck doing paperwork, everybody is giving us a wide berth. We're still in contact with Eve. Mix in the little bombshell you told us about the Serpent being Catherine's grandmother, and you have a nice recipe for disaster. Frankly, I'm amazed we still have a job. So, it's true, you did let them go?" Roy asked. "And before you start, Charles and I discussed this as well and we would have done the same, boss. Not for Alan, I don't give a rat's ass about him. But for Eve, yes."

Tristan smiled. "Thank you, that means a lot. And yes, I did promise to give them as much as a head start, humanly—or better said Company—possible. The Serpent knows, by the way. She is, after all, the greatest seer the world has ever seen. So apparently, she wasn't really shocked by my decision. There's more, though. Eve and Alan were instructed to be there. By the Serpent. And good thing they were. You see, Catherine died during the blast."

Roy and Charles stared at him.

"Come again, sir?" Charles eyebrows almost touched the ceiling.

"Yes, she did," he softly replied. "I thought I was going to lose it. Eve actually slapped me across the face to pull me out of it." Tristan stared into nothing. "Anyway," he said, pulling himself back to the here and now, "Eve was there to revive her. Also, with her temporary death, Catherine's power of being a master of death, transferred back to Alan."

Roy rolled his eyes. "Oh goody! What fun! Alan has his destructive power back. Like he needed any more of that."

Tristan pinched the bridge of his nose. "Roy, please. Not now, man. I'm not a fan, either, but we have to give Eve the benefit of the doubt here. If she trusts him, so will I."

Roy looked at Charles. "I hope you don't mind my keeping a close eye on him, but fair enough."

"Shame we were out cold by the blast at that point," Charles said.

Tristan hesitated. "Yes...about that. You weren't exactly knocked out by the blast. Like I said, nobody was supposed to know Catherine died. So, Alan sort of, well, he told you guys to take a nap. For the record, I was seriously displeased by his actions."

Roy stood up and started pacing the room. "That son of a bitch! Oh, if I ever get my hands on that guy." He made a strangling gesture with his hands.

Tristan sighed. "You'll do no such thing, and you know it. Then again, I probably wouldn't stop you. Mind you, Eve would." He looked at Charles. "You look awfully calm, Charles. This doesn't upset you?"

"Upset me? No, not really, sir. I find it mildly irritating. I was actually more concerned with the extent of his empathic powers. I didn't even see him, so he doesn't need eye contact to make someone fall asleep at will. That's a pretty nifty power, wouldn't you agree?"

Tristan looked at him. "I don't know, Charles. I hadn't really thought about it. Yes, I guess it is."

"Could you?" Roy asked.

"Without eye contact? I don't know. I don't think I ever tried. Why would I?"

"Well, no time like the present. Let's get this show on the road. Give it your best shot, boss," Roy said, while moving towards the sofa in the room and facing away from Tristan.

He had to laugh. "Are you sure you want to play guinea pig, Roy?"

"Hit me, boss."

Tristan focused his powers on Roy and commanded him in his mind to go to sleep. Immediately Roy sank to the ground, missing the sofa by an inch with a loud thump.

"Wow!" Charles cried out and moved over to Roy.

"Damn, that has got to hurt," Tristan said and focused again. "Wake up," he said out loud this time. Roy opened his eyes.

"Ouch! So, it worked?" Roy asked, rubbing the back of his head. "So much for my ability to drop to the floor with grace."

"Hmm, it would be interesting to see if you could still do this outside of the office. Or with more people in the room," Charles remarked.

Roy, still rotating his head from left to right, trying to ease the pain, looked at Charles. "Perfect. Let's get some of the younger folks in the gym. I'm done, thank you very much."

Both Charles and Tristan laughed.

"I'm sure it's worth finding out how far my powers would stretch, but I wouldn't call it a high priority right now. We've got bigger things to worry about. Like, what is going to happen today and what about this whole ball drop event?"

"And is Kate going to blow up the entire Company once she finds out her grandmother is still alive?" Roy put in.

"And then, there's that, yes." Tristan sighed. "Like I said, we've got bigger things to worry about."

"Sir, don't you think the time has come to pay Miss Catherine a visit?" Charles asked.

"I've thought about it, Charles. Really, I have. I'm actually considering dropping by later today. It's her birthday. Honestly, though, I have no idea what to do. It's been weeks now since my demotion and we're still here, so I don't think they are going to fire us anytime soon. Furthermore, I do think the Serpent needs me. At least where Catherine is concerned, but is it worth the risk? I don't want to jeopardize your chances here in the company. Not because of something I did."

"Very admirable, sir, but we can take care of ourselves, can't we, Roy?" Charles asked.

"Well, duh," Roy said, rolling his eyes. "Besides, boss, I honestly don't know if I want to stay here if they sack you. I'm sure MI5 would love to have a guy like me and who wouldn't want this old tosser working for them?" Roy said, slapping Charles on the back.

"Much obliged, I'm sure," Charles replied dryly. "What Roy is so eloquently trying to say, sir, is that you shouldn't worry about us. We like working for you, yes, but as stated just now, we can hold our own."

"I'd worry more about showing up on her doorstep without a present," Roy said casually.

Tristan looked at him. "That, my friend, is an excellent point. And I have just the thing. I think a trip to my safety deposit box is in order," and he left without an explanation.

Alan

I'm used to *getting what I want. For a long time, what I wanted, was Catherine. Kate, to me. Now, there someone else in my life. She's almost the opposite of her. I like it. This may be hard to believe for a man my age, but Kate was my first, true love. Yes, I tried to manipulate her. More than I care to remember because leaving me was not an option. I would have done anything for her. I was willing to give up my most coveted power for her. I did. It backfired. I never blamed her, but it did give me a clean slate, so to speak. My love for her was obsessive. I see that now. Today, someone else is doing the manipulating. I know what my Kate can do and I will never make the mistake of underestimating her again. I got your stupid painting in, Serpent, now you have fun with it. I certainly hope you know what you're doing.*

"Ah, we've reached the middle of the North Atlantic. On a bright day like this, it does offer an amazing view, don't you think?" Beatrice Fletcher looked at her flying companions. Alan saw Eve look through one of the round, little windows.

"It is rather humbling, isn't it?" she said to Beatrice.

The older lady smiled. "You took the words right out of my mouth, dear. Now, would you care for some tea?"

Eve smiled. "Tea would be lovely."

Beatrice stood up to talk to the purser they had on board. "I'm just going to go check and see he doesn't forget the biscuits and sandwiches. I brought them aboard especially for you, and it would be just like Gary to forget all about them, bless his heart."

George Fletcher, reading the paper, gave his wife's hand a soft squeeze while she passed him. "You do that, honey."

Thankfully, Alan had been left to his own devices for a good deal of the flight. George Fletcher was a pleasant man, but not a big talker and he liked to read. Every now and then, he would comment on an article, asking Alan's opinion. Alan pretended to be reading a book himself. It was a small sacrifice to get to New York this fast and, more importantly, undetected. Though perhaps not from the Serpent herself, but Alan figured she had bigger things to worry about.

Eve had the short end of the deal, in his opinion. Beatrice Fletcher was a kind-hearted, lovely woman, to be sure, but by god, did she ever shut up? Alan had been watching Eve with rising respect for her patience by the hour. Of course, Eve was a mind reader, so it was quite easy for her to redirect the conversation to topics she found harmless or, at least, agreeable. Though he seriously doubted she took any pleasure in being made aware of the latest knitting patterns. He knew she could pick up on his thoughts as well and sometimes noticed her smile when he mentally rolled his eyes at something Beatrice had said.

He laid down the book and took a peek outside the window as well. It was a rather beautiful view. An almost clear sky with one or two fluffy white clouds moving through the sky like sheep. From this point of view, it always seemed like the clouds would hold their weight and they could just drift along through the sky. Wouldn't that be something? He sighed. Kate had levitated him once, using her power of air, just so he could experience the feeling. He would never forget that glorious moment of weightlessness. The memory made him smile.

Kate. Today was her thirty-sixth birthday. They'd been together for more than seven years. First, quite sneakily, because back then, even though Kate had already graduated, it was still frowned upon to begin a relationship with a former student. She had caught his eye the moment she walked into his classroom, and he'd practically jumped through the ceiling with excitement. An elemental in his classroom. A real elemental. Alan, besides being an empath and a master of death, also had the ability to recognize other people with powers or abilities. And he'd never come across someone with that much power. She'd practically lit up the room. Not that she had any idea. Catherine had always been a down-to-earth kind of person. A wicked sense of humour, which had appealed to him more than anything, and she had a high self-esteem, which he liked. He hated insecure women. He was not the knight in shining armour type and he certainly wasn't the share your feeling kind of man. From his experience, insecure women always wanted to talk about feelings. And not even about their own feelings, no his. On and on. Of course, as a professional psychologist he'd had to put up with a lot of women who fit this description.

He looked at Eve. She was magnificent. Every human being had their insecurities, to be sure, but Eve oozed confidence everywhere she went. Plus, she was absolutely drop-dead gorgeous. Alan was not an idiot; he did see the similarities. It was almost like Kate and Eve were two different sides of the same coin. Both self-assured, powerful women, both waist-long hair, though Kate's hair was a bit longer.

He wondered what had attracted Eve to Tristan. He'd met Tristan face-to-face three times now. First at the abandoned underground, to explain that Kate had all the necessary ingredients to defeat that bloody asteroid. Something he thought she would have picked up on almost immediately, but apparently, he'd overestimated her in that aspect. It still stung that Kate had really believed he would have killed her. He'd gotten under Tristan's skin. He knew that, and, quite honestly, it had felt good. Truth was, Alan had been quite intimidated with Tristan's powers. Sure, normally he could have destroyed him in the blink of an eye and he still could have, even without the power of being a master of death. Alan had known in an instant that was where they were very different from one another. Tristan hated taking lives. Not that he, Alan, rejoiced at the idea, but he certainly didn't shy away from it, either. If someone was pure evil and got in his way, well, they should have stayed out of his way. He did what needed to be done.

Second time was when Kate got hit by the blast of the asteroid, which had dissolved into god knows what, leaving her for dead on the ground. That was when he realised Tristan truly loved his Kate. Tristan had been frantic, and Eve had slapped him across the face. He smiled. That had been a good moment. He had to give him credit, though. Tristan did let them go. He knew it had been for Eve's benefit, but nonetheless, he had given them a head start, at personal expense. Eve had made it perfectly clear the Company would give him a very hard time, and Tristan had even been demoted. Not that he cared about that. Much. Maybe a bit, because of Eve.

He had been fascinated with the extent of Tristan's powers, though. Alan could sense someone's abilities and Tristan's empathic ones had been off the chart. He'd never seen anything like it, and that most certainly included his own. The difference between them was Tristan would probably never use the more colourful, dangerous part of his powers. So, in a strange way, he and Eve coveted the same quality and apparently had looked for it in their partners. Goodness. Light, Kate would say. In a one-on-one combat he, Alan, would win, of course. There was no doubt in his mind about that. He'd never met another master of death, although he suspected he probably could have trained Meg, one of Kate's friends, to become one. It slumbered inside of her. Meg was too soft, though. What a waste.

Even without it, he would probably win. Alan knew how to play dirty and the extent of his powers. Tristan most certainly did not. He only thought he did. *Tristan could probably knock down an entire square full of people with one single thought*, he mused. Shame the Company focussed on their so-called clients. Eve had told him about the Company's training program and he found it lacking. Sure, they required their agents to be in excellent health, and they did test their abilities. But other than that, it sounded like the regular MI5, FBI, CIA program. Perhaps a bit closer to NSA or KGB style, but not by much.

He would add an entire section to schooling their own agents. Learning more about their abilities to make better use of them. Increase them, even, where ever possible. Eve had laughed when he'd made a comment about that.

"Do you think it's a stupid, idea?" he'd asked.

She'd shaken her head. "No, not at all, but you have to realise, the Company is, in fact, a company. It's not a school, university or even a training program. We're just a bunch of employees. Yes, with special abilities and we do get the occasional training, just like you would at any other company and the staying in shape part can be tough, but we are not their main focus. The people we have to protect or bring down are our main focus."

"I still think there's room for improvement there," Alan had replied.

"Be my guest and explain your views to the Serpent, love. I'm sure they would be more than happy to see you walk through the front door." She had looked at him with a rather devious smile and he'd chased her around the room, both ending up on the bed, laughing.

He remembered the last time he'd met Tristan. It was just before they decided to go for the Lake District and ended up in the B&B where they'd met George and Beatrice. They had stayed in London for too long. He'd known that, but Eve had been hesitant to leave. She felt leaving would make it final. Leaving behind the life she'd known and the people she cared about.

Tristan had chased him through half of London, but Alan felt his heart hadn't been in it. It had been just for show. Still, he'd had to stay focussed the entire time because Tristan's powers as an empath had not been his only concern. Tristan was fast and most definitely in excellent condition. Alan's condition was getting better now they were "on the run." Being in a comatose state of mind for years had left his muscles almost non-existent. The hospital had made sure his legs and arms had a certain exercise workout, so he hadn't lost completely everything, but even he had to admit he had mostly to thank the Company for his body's current shape. Not that it had been painless, but at least he could walk. Run even, as their latest escape had proved.

He looked at Eve. A ray of sunlight touched her face and lit up her eyes. That was probably the last similarity between Kate and Eve. Both had very special eyes, though even Alan had to admit Kate could not compete in that particular department. He'd never seen such beautiful eyes as the first time he looked into Eve's. The moment his life began again; the moment she had revived him. Her face, her eyes were the first things he'd seen, and for a moment he had been sure he was actually dead and maybe even in Heaven, by some miraculous mistake. They were lilac, a light purple with a glow when the sun would light up her features, like they did right now. A mutation, she had said to him, and the remark had made him sad. Kate had said the same about her green eyes. A mutation. Apparently, he was a sucker for mutants. Should probably try to locate professor Charles Xavier. Maybe he could drop by the Company as well to tell them they were completely and utterly lacking in their training program. He noticed Eve tried to hide a smile. She'd probably picked up on his latest train of thought.

He smiled at her and picked up his book when Beatrice came over, Gary on her heels, with a tray of sandwiches and more.

"George, put that paper down and come and entertain our guests."

Catherine

"Kate! Someone's at the door. Do you want me to get it?" Leah yelled from the living room, her hands full of cookie dough she just took out of the fridge.

Catherine came running down the stairs. "Nope, I'll get it. Who is it?"

Leah looked up. "Don't know. It's on this floor, so probably one of your neighbours. They can't borrow any sugar. We're almost out ourselves as it is," she yelled after Kate.

Kate raised her hand to acknowledge she'd heard Leah's comment and went into the hallway and opened the door.

"Tristan," she said, completely taken aback.

"Hello, birthday girl. Can I come in?" he asked. The phrasing was innocent enough, but Catherine felt the weight behind his question wash over her. He really was asking her permission to come inside.

"Of course," she replied, thoughts flying through her mind. Was it safe to talk? Were they listening? Was he here on company orders? Dammit, how could she know? She stepped aside to let him pass, but Tristan stopped and raised his hand to touch her cheek and looked deep into her eyes.

"I've missed you," he said. Before Catherine could reply, his lips were on hers and he pulled her closer. The moment their lips connected Catherine felt safe, secure, loved, protected. This was Tristan, letting her know it was okay to talk. She sighed and prolonged the kiss, not wanting to let go just yet.

"I've missed you, too," she said and sighed.

"*Tutto a suo tempo, miei elementi,*" he whispered in her ear. Catherine shivered.

"Well, I think *this* is a very good time, Tristan." She took him by the hand and led him through the living room towards the kitchen.

"Lee, you suck. Your powers are completely off-kilter. Say hello to Tristan."

Leah dropped the bowl she was holding, which was fortunately made out of plastic and landed on the kitchen floor, bowl still intact.

"*Godgloeiendego…,*" Leah started to say, when she pulled herself together.

"Tristan, how nice of you to drop by. Unannounced. Completely unexpected. Next time, be a dear and give me a heads up?"

Tristan laughed and came over to give Leah a hug. "So sorry, Leah, this was a spur of the moment decision. I'm sure you're not dropping the ball. Oh, bad choice of words! Again, so sorry, you know what I mean, right?"

Leah sighed and shook her head. "Yes, Tristan, I know what you mean. I do have some interesting news on that front, by the way. Or rather, worrying news, but at least it's news. I'm sure, however, you two lovebirds have plenty of catching up to do and I still have to check us in for our flight tomorrow, so I'm going to get out of your hair and I'll call back in an hour when the party starts?"

Leah didn't even wait for a reply and grabbed her purse and coat. "Kate, set the oven to one hundred and sixty degrees. They will need twelve to thirteen minutes to bake properly. They are all set to go. Don't leave them on the counter. They will go soggy. Bye, Tristan!" She waved before closing the front door behind her.

"Wow, subtle," Catherine said. "Want to help me get these on a tray?" She pointed at the cookies. "Shame to let them go to waste, and I'll never hear the end of it."

Tristan smiled. "Sure. Does she really have to check you in?"

Catherine looked at him. "Seriously? You even have to ask? Of course not. She just wanted to give us some alone time, in her own not so subtle way. And how do you know we're travelling? Silly question. Don't answer that. I don't even want to know."

"Wow, hang on. Catherine, I want you to know we took everything down here, no Company equipment left. Scout's honour." He raised his hand in the air.

"But?" Catherine asked.

"Well, we do have the ability to hack into anything, anytime we please," he added rather sheepishly.

"Right," she replied, putting the last cookie on the tray. "Okay, these are good to go, I think." She opened the oven door and pushed the tray inside. "Twelve to thirteen minutes and counting. Want something to drink?"

"What are you having?" Tristan asked.

She shrugged. "Well, I just had coffee, but I think I could actually use a glass of wine."

He looked at her. "Do you have any Prosecco?"

"I think so, yes."

He continued. "Limoncello? Ice cubes? Mint perhaps?"

Catherine raised an eyebrow. "Umm, I might have Limoncello in the freezer. I'm not sure actually. Why?"

"I'd like to make a Limoncello Spritz for you. It will go nicely with the present I have for you."

"Oh," So he'd bought her a present. Was that the real reason he was here, though? She could tell he was really happy to see her, but it had been weeks and not as much as a peep. She had to wonder what had changed.

Tristan looked at her.

"You're worried about something. What is it?"

"I was wondering why you're here. Now, I mean. Why not sooner? Why not later? Or are you really just dropping by because it's my birthday?"

Tristan took two glasses out of her cabinet, having found both Limoncello and ice cubes. Catherine automatically turned around to cut some mint from the herbal section of plants in her kitchen and handed it to him.

While he poured a third of Limoncello in the glass, he answered her question. "Of course, I wanted to be here, or anywhere with you for that matter, sooner rather than later. If I could have done so safely, I would have, Catherine. I hope you believe that."

She felt his hesitation. He added two thirds of Prosecco to their glasses.

"There's been a…development at the company. I'm not sure if it's a good thing, though. I gave my word not to reveal anything until after your birthday. And I won't. However, this is you we're talking about, and I don't trust that blasted painting."

Catherine waited for him to say anything else because she felt his unease and knew there was something more to the story.

"I'm not sure I trust the Company either, Catherine. I would like to give them the benefit of the doubt, but lately I've been struggling with that little phrase which I'm sure is familiar to you. For the greater good."

Her breath hitched. Yes, she was very familiar with that phrase. Alan had used it plenty of times to condone his actions.

Tristan added the mint and handed her one of the glasses. "Can we go sit in the living room? At least till the cookies are done?"

"Sure," she replied and led the way. After he sat down right beside her, he took a jewellery box out of his inner pocket and gave it to her.

"Happy birthday, Catherine," he said softly.

He was giving her a piece of jewellery? *Oh, dear God, what if it's a ring? What if it's not? Would it matter? No. Don't be ridiculous.* Yes, she loved him and deep down she knew he loved her as well, but Tristan would never give her a ring after a couple of months, nor would she want him to. Her fingers were fumbling with the lock on the lid, but she finally managed to open it.

It was a golden bracelet. In the middle there was a big, red gemstone. A ruby. She would recognise that stone anywhere, it was the same colour as both her ring and necklace. Same cut as the necklace even. It was magnificent. And probably very expensive. Oh dear. How to react to such a beautiful gift?

"Do you like it?" he asked.

She could hear the nerves in his voice. "I love it, Tristan. It is so beautiful, but it must have cost a small fortune. How can I possibly accept such a gift?"

"I can honestly say I did not spend a penny. Not that I wouldn't have, by the way, but I had this for many years now. It's my mother's. After she became a diabetic, her wrists grew thicker and my father offered to have it enlarged by a goldsmith, who's a friend of the family, but instead she gave it to me. She said I would know to which special lady it belonged to when the time came. And she was right. I did know. I want you to have it and I hope it will give you as much pleasure as it gave my mother."

She felt tears in her eyes. "I don't know what to say. Thank you. I feel honoured, truly. I will wear it with pride. Will you put it on me?" She held out the box, and he took the bracelet, putting the box on the side table.

"Hold out your arm." He put the bracelet on her wrist, and they heard the lock connect to the little magnetic part, build in as extra security. He pulled her close, and she automatically put her arms around his neck. She felt warm again and protected. Underneath it, though, there was something else. Worry? Anxiety? He was definitely worried about something. Probably her because it did not feel like it had anything to do with Tristan himself. Catherine reached out to her earth element to soothe and ground him. She felt him relax against her body. He pulled back a little and smiled at her.

"You don't have to do that, you know."

She smiled back. "I know, but I like to. It's the least I can do. Besides, I want you to feel safe as well. You're not leaving anytime soon, are you?"

He caressed her cheek with the palm of his hand. "Not today, no. Today I'm all yours," he said before he kissed her, and she felt fire inside her starting to burn. She had trouble breathing because of the amount of passion that washed over her when a beeping noise pulled her back to reality.

"The cookies are done," she whispered. She heard Tristan mumble something in Italian that she was pretty sure would not be in their dictionary and let out a giggle.

"What is it you said to me? *Tutto a suo tempo?*" she said and heard him laugh.

"Wow, you can never say anything about my Dutch accent. Ever. But the words are correct, yes. Well, let's go save your bloody cookies then." He stood up and reached out his hand to Catherine.

"Yes, sir!" she replied, sticking out her tongue and sprinted towards the kitchen. "Last one there doesn't get a cookie!"

Eve

"Okay, so it's very probable they are fully booked, but we really need to get a room in this hotel, Alan, so full force, if you please," Eve whispered to Alan. They were standing in front of the High Line hotel in Chelsea, New York. Roy had texted them the girls were staying at the Wellington Hotel and Catherine and Deborah would be staying at Leah and Ryan's place.

After some debate, they had decided it would probably be better to stay close to wherever Catherine would be, so they'd looked for hotels around West Twenty-Second Street, where Leah lived. Alan had declared the Savoy too far away, so they decided to go for the High Line Hotel instead, which was basically just one block away.

Eve stepped through the door first with Alan hot on her heels. She determinately walked up to the front desk, a dazzling smile in place.

"Welcome to the High Line Hotel, how may I help you?" The young man behind the front desk looked more than willing to help them. Eve tuned in to the thoughts in his mind and immediately found out he was very pleased with her looks. Not so much that she was with a companion, but she could feel Alan's powers at work and the young man visibly relaxed.

"Hello. We're fine, thank you. A bit tired after such a long flight. My name is Eve and this is my older brother, Alan. We came here as fast as we could. Our mom was hospitalised, you see, and we couldn't leave her on her own for New Years', so we hopped on the first flight out and here we are. Thing is, we don't have a reservation." She sighed. "I know, right? Completely clueless for this time of year, but we were in such a hurry, we totally forgot. I don't suppose you could help us out?

The cost doesn't matter," she finished with another dazzling smile.

So, it's her brother! Well, that's good. God, she's gorgeous. Nice as well, dropping everything to visit their mom. Are we fully booked? Maybe the suite, which had been cancelled this morning? Bit expensive, though, but if money really isn't an issue? Eve made sure to keep a straight face, looking slightly concerned while she listened to his thoughts. They were in!

"Well, it looks like you're in luck. We've just had a cancellation for our High Line suite. I have to be honest, though, it's in our higher price range." He handed her the list to point out the costs.

Eve didn't even blink an eye. "That would be perfect! Alan, you don't mind bunking with your kid sister, right?"

Alan smiled at her and tousled her hair. "As long as you don't snore anymore."

She rolled her eyes at the young man. "He's always teasing me."

The lobby attendant laughed as well. "I will get everything in order for you. Could I have both your passports, please?"

Eve handed over both their passports. She could feel an enormous wave coming from Alan and for a moment wondered what he was doing, as she had her full focus on the young man, currently writing down their details and visibly pleased he'd just rebooked their most expensive room.

"If you would both sign here at the bottom? And can I have your credit card? It won't be charged until you leave. So, you'll be staying until the new year?"

"Yes," Eve replied while Alan signed first. With her own surname, she noticed. So that's what he had been doing. Impressive bit of mind control. "We're not sure when we're flying back, though. Is that a problem?" she asked.

"Not at all, miss. If you can let us know when you'll be leaving one day in advance, that would be perfect."

"Of course."

He handed them back their passports and Eve's credit card.

"So, this is the key card to your room. You're on the top floor." He pointed out on a hotel map how to get there and also handed them a brochure. "I don't know if you're familiar with our history, but this hotel has quite a few details you might want to check out. Some even in your own room." He smiled at her. "We serve exquisite coffee at our Intelligentsia. For food and drinks, you can either visit our Alta Linea restaurant or our lobby bar if you'd like a late-night snack." He highlighted when breakfast was served and asked if they needed help with their luggage.

Eve shook her head. "No, thank you. We'll be fine. You've been most helpful. Alan, shall we go upstairs?" Alan smiled at the lobby attendant and took Eve's luggage as well. Not that is was a lot. They both had a carry-on with them and personal belongings. Alan's personal items were in his man-bag, which also contained his laptop and Eve herself was carrying a large handbag. Once the lift doors had closed behind them, Alan grinned at her.

"Older brother?"

Eve laughed. "Well, some hotels can be difficult about unmarried couples. Besides, he really liked me. You being with me nearly broke his heart, honey. Couldn't let that happen, now could I?" Then she playfully wacked him over the head. "And I do not snore!"

Alan grinned. "You so do. Don't worry. I don't mind. It's a cute snore."

Eve rolled her eyes at him and got out on the top floor. It was completely deserted, which was probably normal, considering the time of day. People would be out and about exploring the city.

"This is us, I believe." She opened the door and whistled. "I think I can manage here for the next couple of days." It was a spacious room, with one big king bed and a separate sitting area. Books decorated the room, as well as some well-chosen rugs on the floor and a lovely mantelpiece, although the blazing days of the fireplace beneath it seemed to be over. All in all, it had a very homey vibe, a bit European even. Eve liked it. She looked at Alan, who obviously approved as well.

"What is the plan? Try to find out as much as we can about the actual ball drop?" Alan asked.

Eve took two glasses and poured them a drink from the well-stocked minibar. "I think that would aid Tristan and his team, let alone Cathe… I mean Kate, the best. I think it's safe to say the Company is sort of flying blind without intel from the Serpent. He is, after all, their most prized seer. Even if nobody knows he is actually a she. From what I understand, they are pretty much left in the dark. Maybe because Kate's grandmother is focussing on her grand reveal, maybe this is all going exactly according to her plans and maybe she's losing her touch. Honestly, it's hard to tell from a distance. If we stick to the facts, however, that ball is definitely going to drop too fast. In my book, that's a bad thing."

She saw Alan smile. "What?' she asked before she picked it up in his mind. "Ooh! Well, yes, I do trust Leah's abilities. Or, more accurately, I trust Tristan's judgement. If he says she a very good seer, then she's a very good seer. And if you must know, I'm actually quite fond of her books."

Alan laughed. "I'll take your word for it. She wrote them while I was sleeping, so to speak. I'll add them to my wish list then," he said and gave her a wink. "Seriously, though, the ball drop sounds like a good place to start. I did some research on the plane."

Eve nodded. "Yes, I know. I'm glad you got some time to plan ahead. Beatrice is nice and I'm very grateful they got us here so fast, but I'm quite drained, if I'm being absolutely honest." Alan looked at her, concern in his eyes. "Oh, nothing to fret about, love. It'll pass. Nothing a good night's sleep won't cure. What did you find out?"

He opened his MacBook and showed her the screen. "Look. There are two major organisations involved when it comes to the ball drop. The Times Square Alliance and Countdown

Entertainment. Then obviously we'll have to deal with the NYPD on the day itself. Times Square is closed off in the beginning of the late afternoon. The entire square will be divided into what they call "pens" and security will be tight. A famous person usually assists with the actual ball drop by pressing the button. Just for your information, this is not what activates the drop. That is done from a control room, synchronized using a government time signal. This year it is rumoured that Billie Eilish will perform John Lennon's "Imagine" and assist with the ball drop. There will be other artists performing in the hours leading up to New Year's."

Eve had been leaning over and stretched her back. "Okay. So, the actual ball is set in motion from a control room. Do we know where that is?"

Alan shook his head. "No, it's something we can look into ourselves or ask Tristan's team to look into it. A quick search on the Internet doesn't reveal much about the location of the control room nor the location of the special panels which are made each year for the ball."

"Panels?" Eve asked. She vaguely remembered something about a theme but wasn't quite sure where she'd read that.

Alan looked away from his screen and turned around to face her. "Yes. Since twenty fourteen a theme has been added to the event. Each year a different theme is chosen and then brought to life on these crystal panels by a guy named Tom Brennan and his team of Waterford Crystal, an Irish company. Their company is also responsible for the chandeliers in Westminster Abbey."

"So, they're probably very busy dotting the i's, one could assume."

Alan smiled. "One could, but one shouldn't." He turned back to the screen and scrolled down. "Here. *The panels are kept at One Times Square, in the building with the Walgreens at the bottom. We ship in the new panels on whatever airline is flying that day. We have special containers. Then they are kept in a secret location in New York*

City, and we make sure that they are completely guarded until they are ready to be used. This year, on Dec. 27, our engineers installed them onto the ball. This was from an interview with Tom Brennan late twenty eighteen. I think it's safe to say they still follow the same procedure, more or less anyway. The whole thing has to be up and running before six p m. though because that's when they will officially light up the ball and raise it to the top for the drop. If someone is planning an act of terrorism, they will have to do it before six p.m. At least, I think that would make the most sense. Leah didn't see an object crashing into the ball or anything. She saw the ball dropping way too fast. So, it's a realistic assumption someone will attempt to sabotage the event, right?"

Eve gave him a hug. "Good work, honey. And, yes, I think you're on the right track here. I'm also leaning towards sabotage. To what extent, that has yet to be determined. Which is what has me worried the most, actually. People have had a bad year and they are on edge. Viruses, a freaking asteroid, this has not been a good year for planet Earth. This will probably be one of the first major events where people will stand united to celebrate the new year. Everybody is very much looking forward to a new year, I think. Out with the old, in with the new, now more than ever. If someone wants to hurt as many people as possible, the New York ball drop sounds like the perfect place to do some serious damage."

"I have not survived the almost-end-of-the-world to have some idiot screw it up now."

She could hear the anger in his voice. "Easy, love. I'm sure we'll figure it out. It might just be a malfunction. Which could turn out pretty dangerous in itself, but maybe there's nothing more to it."

Alan looked at her. "But you don't really believe that, do you? I can feel your doubt."

She sighed. "No. I don't really believe that. Besides, my motto is: prepare for the worst, then things can only get better."

Alan smiled. "I like that motto. It's sensible."

Eve laughed. "Really? Normal people would say it's a gloomy way of thinking."

"We're not normal people," he replied.

"No, we're not. How do you want to approach this? Are we going to split up and go solo or are we teaming up?"

Alan turned away from the screen again to face her, and Eve could hear his thoughts spinning. "I think we might need our combined powers when it comes to a conversation with the Times Square Alliance. Then I could convince them we're NYPD, and you could listen to what they're actually thinking. Maybe there is something they normally wouldn't say." He looked at Eve, who nodded her approval and then continued. "When it comes to Countdown Entertainment, either you or I could go solo, but frankly, this would be a way easier job for someone like Leah or even Deborah. Leah is a celebrated New York author, for God's sake. Her books are about to hit the big screen. I'm sure they'll be happy to see her. Deborah could accompany her. After all, she knows a lot of people in the music business. They could just pretend to have an interest in the whole ball drop event and use Leah's fame to get them special tickets or something."

Eve frowned. "I'm not sure Kate would like that plan very much. Involving her friends in something potentially dangerous?"

Alan snorted. "You obviously don't know Kate like I do. Yes, she's a force for good, but by god, that woman has a gift for looking for trouble. Though she would probably argue trouble usually finds her."

"Still, won't she think we're using her friends for something potentially dangerous?"

He shook his head. "No, I don't think so. Kate values honesty. I think if we explain why we need them, she'll think it makes sense. And Leah will certainly want to help. Didn't Tristan say this whole ball drop vision has her extremely annoyed?" He looked at her.

"Hmm, yes. Tristan did text she was rather vexed about not seeing more." Eve picked up something in Alan's mind. "Oooh, that's a very interesting train of thought, love. You think Leah isn't seeing more details because the people involved haven't made up their minds."

Alan smiled. "It's a theory, Eve. Just a theory, but yes. I thought it would make sense a seer would only see things when people have decided to follow through on something. Don't they always say; the future isn't set? I think that's because we constantly change our minds. Humans, I mean. Pesky free will and all that." He winked at her.

"Well, I suppose it couldn't hurt to ask, right? You want to try the Times Square Alliance today?" She didn't feel like it, but Eve was never one for skipping responsibilities.

"Honey, not that you're not a true beauty, but you look exhausted. In fact, you look how I feel. Do you really want to go after this right now?"

She shrugged. "Yes, I'm tired. However, you know as well as I do if we try to get some shut-eye right now, we'll definitely be wide awake all night." She looked at Alan, who raised an eyebrow and she had to laugh. "Yes, I'm sure you don't see that as a bad thing, but we really need some sleep as well." She gave him a punch in the shoulder.

"Ouch! Be careful with my delicate muscles and bones, woman," he teased her.

"I'll remember that tonight and leave you alone. Nothing restores the body so well as a good night's sleep, after all." She looked at him with her most innocent smile. It worked. He looked at her with a slight hint of faked panic.

"No, no, I'm good." As if putting his words to action, Alan walked towards the door and reached for his coat. "Coming?"

Eve sighed. She had set this in motion, so she'd better not back down now. "Sure, but I want some goddamn coffee first."

"Yes, ma'am. Lead the way."

Tristan

It wasn't exactly a party, but it was a nice gathering of friends. Leah had not returned after an hour, but after four hours and had brought Deborah along with her. Catherine's mother and her new partner, Simon had arrived, along with two other people, a man and a woman, who he guessed would be her uncle and aunt. Tristan had pretended not to notice Catherine's mother staring. She was probably assessing his aura. Catherine had told him once her mother was an expert in reading people's auras and he had no doubt she could. He knew the extent of Catherine's powers and these women obviously came from a very powerful bloodline. Her grandmother was the greatest seer he'd ever met. Probably in the whole world. He'd wager her own mother probably could do more if she put her mind to it, but she seemed content with living a simple, down to earth kind of life. He understood that. Powers could be a blessing and a curse as well. In any case, she seemed to like him and for this, he was grateful. Not that she knew he'd let her daughter die. She'd probably like him a lot less then.

Catherine had asked if Charles and Roy were still part of his team. Once he had confirmed that, she had graciously invited them to come over. He'd hesitated, but eventually gave them a call and Charles had been ecstatic.

Sue was there, as were Sheila, Meg and Harry, Romy and Martin and Joni. He didn't see the twins, though, nor Caroline, Samantha and Helen, who were all part of Catherine's inner circle. Maybe they would be joining the party later. If any of them were surprised to see him there, they didn't let it show. They treated him like an old friend, and Deborah and Leah in particular seemed genuinely pleased to see him again.

"Tristan, we've missed you. Some of us more than others," Deborah said to him, handing him a small cup of coffee. "Espresso, if memory serves me correctly?"

He smiled at her. "You remembered. Thank you, Deborah. It's a pleasure seeing you again as well. How have you been?"

Deborah laughed. "You mean, how's Kate been doing, but thank you for asking anyway. It was a good choice, leaving the cello behind. It immediately put her mind at ease. At least about your feelings for her. Of course, she did worry about your well-being. As for me, I'm doing pretty well, actually. I took a few weeks off in November to spend time with my kid brother back in the Netherlands. Romy filled in for me and even Meg pitched in, so I could have more time with him. How are you?" she asked with speculative eyes.

"That's nice, Deborah. I'm happy for you you've got to spend time with your family. I still have to visit my parents back in Italy. I never got around to it. And for the record, though I always love to hear about Catherine, I was honestly asking how you are doing. I'm glad to hear you're doing well. I'm doing a lot better now I've seen Catherine, but I don't mind saying these last couple of weeks weren't exactly the best of my life."

"Hmm, we figured as much. They did not fire you, did they?" She had a frown on her face, and he could feel her concern.

"No, they need me too much to fire me. And you shouldn't concern yourself with my career, Deborah. Trust me, I can hold my own."

She shrugged. "I'm sure you can, but we sort of felt responsible. I hope the letter did some good."

Letter? What letter? "I'm not sure I know what you mean."

"Oh, I thought Catherine would have told you by now," she said sheepishly. "Well, it was Leah's idea, you see. You gave her your business card. She'd forgotten all about it, but when you didn't show up after the first week, we figured maybe something had gone terribly wrong. So, we looked into ways of finding this Company you work for. That turned out to be rather tricky. Then, after dinner at Leah's place, she suddenly jumped up and went to get her coat. She'd never worn it again after Samhuinn, but she came back with your card." She hesitated.

"And?" he asked, a bit anxious. *What had those silly women done?*

"Well, like I said, Leah came up with the plan to sort of write a letter of recommendation. How we never would have made it without you preparing us for battle, so to speak. I hope we didn't do more damage," she finished, looking a bit anxious.

Tristan laughed. That was so nice of them. He wondered where the letter would have ended up, though. "Hardly, Deborah. It might have done some good. Whom did you address it to, though?"

"Well, we used the address you gave Leah and added 'Letter of recommendation, to Tristan Visconti's boss'. We hoped that would do the trick."

All mail was checked, of course, but he was pretty sure this one would have ended up with Trevor. It surprised him he'd never brought it up. Still, he appreciated the gesture. "That would probably work. My boss never mentioned it, but who knows, your letter might have spared me from further demotion." He gave her a wink because he could sense that made her feel sad. She gave him a hesitant smile.

"I'm so sorry to hear that, Tristan—" she said before he cut her off.

"No need, I swear. All they did was demote me to my original status. You see, I was upgraded for the whole asteroid mission. Like I said, no harm done. And most likely thanks to you ladies. So, thank you." He let her feel his sincerity and she smiled. Relieved this time.

"What are you two discussing so sneakily?" Leah cut in and suddenly he found himself being hugged. He had given her a hug earlier, but that had been his initiative. He liked it and remembered he'd really liked Leah from the start.

"Hello, Leah. Did the booking go well?" he asked with a teasing note to his voice. "We didn't really have a chance to catch up earlier this afternoon, did we? As to what we were discussing. I think if I say, thank you, you silly woman, you'll know what we were talking about."

Her cheeks immediately flushed red. "Ah yes, about that, I do hope it didn't get you in any more trouble. It was supposed to help you." She stopped when Tristan raised his hand.

"Don't. It did, I'm absolutely sure. And the gesture is certainly most appreciated."

She smiled. "Well, in that case, you're very welcome. Now, what took you this long?"

He laughed. "God, you certainly haven't changed one bit. I was going to say sorry we ate all the cookies, but I suddenly don't feel that sorry anymore."

She stuck out her tongue at him. "I thought you looked a bit fatter."

"Ouch! Remind me to stay on your good side." Both Deborah and Leah laughed. "So, are you ladies all packed for the Big Apple?"

Leah rolled her eyes. "Don't get me started. I'm a nervous traveller, ask Kate and Deb here. I think I've repacked my suitcase three times already. I'm driving myself insane. I'm longing to see Ryan after New Year's, though. I don't think we've gone this long without seeing each other, since he moved in with me. He won't be there for the party, but he's coming back to the US in January and then we'll have a whole month together."

Deborah looked at her. "I wouldn't mind packing for you if you need any help, hon. Just don't bite my head off."

Tristan thought she was joking, until he heard Leah's response.

"Ahh, and that's sweet of you, but you know I'll most likely break something and I'd rather it won't be you." She looked at him now. "As I'm sure you've noticed, I can have a bit of a temper. Kate and I have that in common."

Deborah nodded. "They do. Whenever you see one of them upset, run. I mean it, run. Anywhere that's away from them."

Leah gave her a friendly push. "Oh, sod off, we're not that bad."

Deborah mouthed behind her back that it really was that bad.

He felt his body and mind relaxing. They really were pleasing women to be around with. It just added to his love for Catherine. She had great taste in friends. Well, perhaps not always. He still wasn't a fan of Alan, but even he came with useful qualities. He hoped they had found a way to New York by now, but he hadn't heard anything from Eve since the last report from Roy. Which reminded him. "Leah, earlier you said you had some news concerning the ball drop." Her smile disappeared immediately, and he was almost sorry he'd brought it up.

"Yes, I do, but not with Mrs. van Dyk here. That woman can spot an interesting conversation from a mile away, and she's had her eye on you for a while now. You aren't leaving anytime soon, are you?"

He confirmed that he wasn't, meanwhile casually turning his head to look at the various people mingling. When he located Catherine's mother, he honed in on her without looking at her and felt all the feelings a concerned mother would feel. Curiosity, anxiety, protectiveness, also a hint of approval. At least her first impression of him was favourable.

Deborah smiled.

"We made sure we said nothing but good things about you."

He looked at her.

"You're getting better every day, Deborah. Could you sense each emotion?"

She nodded and looked rather smug.

"Yes, I think I got all of them. This whole asteroid affair increased my abilities, I think. Well, at least something good came out of it, right?"

"Oh, I would say a lot of good came out of it," he replied as he saw Catherine walking by, giving him a dazzling smile as she noticed him looking. He heard Deborah giggle. "But that is wonderful, about your powers, I mean. Although I do not think they have increased. It only appears that way to you. You probably just unlocked more of your potential. On both sides?" he asked. He knew Deborah had both emphatic and healing powers or at least the potential to develop them to their full extent.

"Oh! I'm not sure, actually. I've been so ecstatic my empathic abilities have increased, I haven't even tried with my healing powers. You think so?"

He shrugged. "It would make sense. I would definitely explore those as well. Not that you should go looking for injuries, of course, but if they happen to come your way, why not?"

She took him seriously. He could sense that and was pleased. He hadn't known Catherine's friends for very long, but he could already tell the Company would be more than happy to have them on board. All the more reason to keep them away as far as possible, these women deserved to lead a normal life. Well, as normal as humanly possible. He had been worried about coming here. Leah was a seer, after all, what if she saw the link between Catherine and the Serpent? He knew he had taken a huge risk there and had even surprised himself to find out that he didn't care. He would deal with it on the spot. Leah's powers worked differently though, and he had been banking on that. Once she knew something, she could see almost everything. Also, when people changed their minds. However, if she was in the dark, she most likely wouldn't see it. And she most definitely did not know about this. She would, though, soon enough. Tristan had decided he would tell Catherine tonight, given the opportunity. Consequences be damned. He would not make the same mistake twice. He wanted to talk to her about New York and even debated telling her Eve and Alan were probably there as well.

"Thank you for the vote of confidence, Tristan. I will do that. Ah, I see your colleagues have arrived. I'm going to say hello to Roy. I'm sure I'll see you later, Tristan." It wasn't a question, but Tristan nodded and smiled at her anyway. He raised his arm and waived so Charles would see where he was. He was currently kissing Catherine's hand and handing her a big bouquet of red roses. Always the perfect gentleman. Roy gave her a quick hug and then turned his attention to Deborah, who almost dragged him away. Tristan focussed his powers more intently on Deborah this time. Just as he was tuning in to her emotions, Leah pulled him out of it.

"I wouldn't worry about it too much, Tristan. Yes, she likes the way he looks, but Deborah is the romantic type and she knows Roy is kind of a ladies' man. No offense, by the way."

"None taken," he replied, turning his focus away from Deborah. "Besides, that is pretty accurate. In his defence, he would never lead a woman on, but Roy is nowhere near settling down. And that moment may never come for him. There's a reason he likes working for the Company. Roy actually thrives on the action and danger. It's what makes him excel in his work."

"And you don't?" Leah asked with a frown on her face.

Tristan hesitated but decided to answer truthfully. "I used to, yes. For many years. Recent events have changed things for me, though. I never really considered the long-term future. With Eve, it was different, she was a Company women herself. We lived together, we worked together on some projects. There wasn't really much to think about. Eve never wanted children, she had made that perfectly clear and I assumed as much because in our line of work the last thing you want to do is give your enemies more leverage to hurt you. It makes you a liability. With Catherine, everything is different. I've never met anyone like her, but I'm pretty sure she wouldn't like my world. I have to consider that. What do you think, Leah?" He gave her a warm smile.

Leah sighed. "Truthfully? I think you underestimate her. In the sense, what she would be willing to do for you. You might be right about the her not liking the Company part, though. I guess you would know that better than I do. Kate hates double standards, corruption, injustice, that sort of thing. If your organisation works against that, she might put up with a lot. Would you give it up? For her?"

"I might, yes. I've actually considered it after the events of the asteroid, but now is not the time. Also, I think Catherine has a right to know what she would be getting into, so that's something we should discuss together."

She reached out to touch his shoulder. "Tristan, I think she pretty much knows what she would be getting into. You haven't seen her in these last couple of weeks. It's not like she was depressed or anything, more like she had put her life on hold. She knew you would come back. She just didn't know when. This afternoon when you walked into her kitchen and I saw you two, it almost made me cry. It was like someone had turned the light on. She's alive again."

He was shocked. How could he not have realised his absence would have such an effect on her? "I'm so sorry, Leah. I stayed away as long as possible so my people would leave her, and all of you, alone. Well, that was plan, anyway. I never meant to—" He cut off abruptly as he noticed Catherine's mother coming their way. Leah caught on quickly as she turned around in the direction he was looking.

"Leah, dear, would you be so kind to introduce us?" Mrs. van Dyk asked.

"Of course." Leah smiled. "Tristan, I'd like you to meet Kate's mother, Mrs. Elizabeth van Dyk."

"Tristan Visconti, ma'am. It's a pleasure to meet you. And may I add I see where Catherine gets her good looks from?" He gently shook her hand and send out a wave of honesty, truth and love for her daughter, though he had no idea how that would manifest in his aura.

"It's nice to finally meet you as well, Tristan. May I call you Tristan?" she asked, though the emphases on the "finally" did not escape his notice.

"Please do," he replied, giving her a smile.

"You call her Catherine. I like that. Oh, not to worry, dear," she said to Leah, who had just rolled her eyes, "I know you all call her Kate, and she introduces herself that way, but she will always be Catherine to me. Did you know she was named after the empress, Catherine the Great?" She looked at Tristan.

"No, she hasn't got around telling me that." He wanted to keep the conversation going, but she had already continued. "Yes, we were both named after queens. My own mother had a passion for royalty and strong women, I suppose."

He was just starting to think this conversation could turn tricky really quick, with Leah picking up what she wasn't supposed to see. Not right now, anyway. He tried to scan the room to locate Charles, so he could use his blocking powers, when Leah excused herself from the conversation, mumbling something about having heard this story a thousand times. Mrs. van Dyk squeezed her hand and added, "You go and enjoy the party, dear."

She looked at Tristan. "A good girl. She and Catherine have been friends almost forever. She's like my second daughter. I'm pleased she's doing so well."

He agreed, "Leah's a lovely woman. It's a blessing having such good friends. Catherine did mention she felt sad she never really got to know her grandmother. I do apologise. I don't want to bring back bad memories."

"Oh no, not at all. I have very fond memories of my mother. My only regret is that Catherine never really got to know her. She was a formidable woman, you see. From Irish descent, Aisling O'Brien, but married an Englishman. Caused quite the scandal within both families. Of course, she already knew it would turn out the way she wanted. I assume Catherine told you my mother was a seer?"

He nodded. "Yes, she did. Part elemental as well, I believe?"

Mrs. van Dyk seemed to be far away for a moment, but quickly recovered. "Yes, but only the power of fire. And I don't think her power worked the same as they do for my daughter. Catherine is always in control. She doesn't have to ask or control them. They are truly a part of her. At least, that is my opinion, I know she doubts her abilities all the time, even now, after... Well, you know. My mother had great difficulty controlling her power over fire. What they do have in common is it seems being connected to their emotions. Or enhanced, at least. My mother was known for her temper. It was a good thing she married my father. He was a very earthy, grounded sort of man. Did you know Aisling even means 'vision' or 'dream'? Makes you wonder what my own grandmother knew. I never got to know her, though. She died before I was born."

"I'm sorry your own mother was taken away from you all so young," he said. Even though she had done the taking herself, it must have come at a high price. The loss of her family.

"So am I. Catherine was just starting to develop her powers. Although I could tell her stories and guide her as best as I could, I missed my mother terribly. Not just as a mother, but as a teacher as well. She could have explained everything that was happening to her so much better, having been there herself."

"If I may say so, Mrs. van Dyk, I think you did an excellent job. And I will do everything in my power to help and guide her." He let the full force of his sincerity wash over her.

She looked at him. "I believe you will. I know what you can do, Tristan, but I can also see your aura and I have no doubt you truly care about her. It's your profession that has me worried. As I understand it, your line of work can be quite dangerous and I don't want to see Catherine hurt. I don't know how good your covers are, but if someone finds out you care about her, love her, that will make her a target, won't it? And then, on the other hand, what if you yourself get hurt, or worse, killed? I think that would break her." She held up a hand when she noticed he was about to protest. "Oh, I know you'll do everything in your power to prevent that and I'm sure you can think of a lot of situations. It's the things you and your company cannot think of that has me worried. Do you understand that, Tristan? I've seen her broken once. I don't want her to go through that again."

"I perfectly understand you, madam, and comprehend your feelings as well. But I assure you, if there's even the slightest chance of Catherine getting hurt, I'll quit the Company."

She looked at him with a speculative gaze. "You would do that for her?"

He nodded. "Yes. Yes, I would." And especially with what he'd most recently found out.

"She would never let you. You know that, right?"

"What wouldn't I let him do?" Catherine asked, giving her mom a kiss. "You're not giving poor Tristan the third degree, are you?"

Tristan gave her a kiss on the top of her head. "Oh, just comparing notes on how stubborn you can be." He gave her one of his boyish smiles.

"Hmpf, I'm not stubborn at all, am I, Mom?"

"Like you would say, on the advice of counsel, I decline to answer that, my darling girl. And I think it's getting near that time you should cut the cake."

Catherine looked at her watch. It was almost nine o'clock. Her mother was explaining that she had been born precisely at nine p.m. and it had become tradition to cut her cake at the moment of her birth. "When she was young, her father always made her a cake. When he passed away, I took it upon myself to take over that tradition till this day. So, every year I bake a cake for my daughter, with a little theme and up until the glazing and everything. She loves it, don't you, dear?"

Catherine gave her mother a warm smile. "Yes, I do, Mom. It's in one of the guest rooms. I didn't have any room in the fridge, and that room is the coolest. I'll go and get it. Leah, can you come over and help me with the cake?" she yelled at her friend.

Leah came over, abandoning her conversation with Meg and Harry and followed Catherine up the stairs. A sudden feeling of dread washed over him. "She was born at exactly nine p.m.?" he asked Catherine's mother.

She nodded. "Yes. Why do you ask?"

"Would you excuse me for a moment, Mrs. van Dyk?" he asked, not waiting for her answer and following Leah up the stairs.

"Tristan, is something wrong?" he heard her ask but kept on going up the stairs. He started to run when he heard Leah's yell.

"Kate, no! Don't touch it!"

When he turned the corner to storm into the guest room, his worst fears materialised before his eyes. Catherine's hand was touching the painting. No, somehow it was already inside the painting. From the corner of his eye, he watched what he himself wanted to do. Leah made a dive for Catherine to pull her back, but it was too late. The painting seemed to bulge and expand for one moment. By the time he'd reached the painting, Leah was on the ground at his feet, sobbing. Catherine was gone.

Tristan was about to reach out his hand to help Leah stand up, when he heard a terrible scream behind him, piercing through his soul. Catherine's mother had just seen her daughter disappear in a painting.

Alan

"You've been most helpful, Mr. LaBoy, we appreciate your time and cooperation," Alan said as they we're walking back towards the lobby.

"Not at all, Officers, the pleasure was all mine. And should you need anything else, even on the day itself, please don't hesitate to contact me. We all want this to go as smoothly as possible." Mr. LaBoy shook Eve's hand, then Alan's and held the door for them.

They stepped outside the building and turned the first corner they came across. "Okay, we have to get to a quieter section of the city to get rid of these clothes," Eve said, while setting a brisk pace for them both.

"I told you, we should have gone by car."

"No, that would have involved stealing an actual police car. We want to draw as little attention as possible, love. Dammit!" Eve said before she slowed down.

"Excuse me, Officer? I'm trying the find the nearest subway. Where would that be?"

Eve looked at the young man, with a British accent, no less. He was holding an iPhone, probably looking at a map. "That would be the Times Square Forty-Second Street Station," she replied in her most American voice, and she pointed in the right direction, which was behind him.

"Oh, that makes sense," he answered as he turned his phone upside down. Eve repressed an audible sigh. "Cheers! Thank you, Officers. Have a good day." He walked towards the subway station.

"Alan, relax. It was just a stupid tourist. Nothing to worry about," Eve said to him. She glanced sideways and saw him flexing the muscles in his arm. He had been tense the entire hour they had been inside. Something was bothering him, but his mind was in turmoil. She couldn't make heads or tails of it. He was all over the place.

Alan let out a sigh. "I know. The accent had me on edge. He was British and for a moment I thought…"

"You thought the Company had caught up with us. Yes, I know, Alan. I can hear your thoughts, remember? You have got to start trusting my abilities, though, or you'll give us away one of these days."

He frowned. "I do trust your abilities. Unconditionally. I thought you knew that."

"What is it then?" she asked while pointing to two big dumpsters. "Can you sense anyone in this street?"

Alan shook his head. "Not right now, but we have to be quick." He hadn't even finished his sentence, when Eve was already out of her uniform, revealing a black jumpsuit and a short, black leather jacket. Alan followed suit and stuffed the uniform in Eve's sports bag, which she had brought along to the meeting. All done, he visibly relaxed. "Okay, nobody saw us. Now let's get the hell out of here. Maybe we should get a bite somewhere. Not dinner, but just something to nibble on. It's been hours since we last ate on the plane. Even if those scones did pack a punch, it would definitely improve my mood. At least, I hope so. Don't worry, Eve. I know I'm on edge. I can't tell you why. It's not that I don't want to. I just honestly don't know what it is."

Eve smiled reassuringly to him. "It's fine, love. Let's find a pub, or something and get a nice pint of beer and 'something to nibble on' as you put it."

They took the subway as well. In New York, it was still pretty much the fastest way to get across town. Same as London. Alan did like New York. He knew it wasn't the city itself that had him on edge. It was something else. The city that never sleeps.

Amsterdam was so completely different. Well, perhaps not in some ways, but being here Alan thought it came closer to the feeling of Rotterdam. Only bigger. New York was a lot bigger. Everything was big here. Building, parks, hotels, even the freaking food came in extremely large portions. *How did Americans handle Europe?* he wondered.

Eve mentioned she wanted to go to Chelsea Market, and they walked a bit on the High Line, whatever that was, but he was happy to follow her around. He knew she was carefully keeping tabs on his thoughts and he didn't mind. It was even kind of nice to have someone who could provide some new insights he hadn't thought of himself. Eve was very easy company. She left him to his own devices, but offered help when he needed it. The meeting had been pretty much useless. In the sense, they hadn't heard anything out of the ordinary. The ball was all set and ready. Nothing strange or notable. The artists had been confirmed, the mayor had been instructed, security had been upgraded and as far as he could tell, every word had been sincere. If there was an insider, he sure as hell didn't know about it, nor had he any reason to suspect anyone.

This worried him. Alan hated variables. He liked to be in total control. Something he actually had in common with Kate. She could improvise, for sure, but she hated not being in control.

Eve informed him they had to exit the subway. He nodded and got up. He enjoyed the short walk on the High Line, which turned out to be a former New York Central Railroad spur on the west side of Manhattan, completely renovated with art and nature everywhere you looked. If he hadn't been so hungry, he would have enjoyed the scenery more. It was like nature had found a way to embrace industrial architecture and they looked happily married. Even the sun peeked through the clouds every now and then, and, absentmindedly, he took a few snapshots of Eve, admiring a piece of art. They took the stairs and reached Chelsea Market. Alan immediately took a shine to it. He noticed Eve smile.

"I had a feeling this would be your thing. It's very popular, but not in an annoying, way-too-busy kind of way."

Alan looked around. "There's so much of everything. You obviously know it better than I do. Do you want to go to anywhere in particular?"

She shrugged. "Not really. I thought we could get a nice cider at the bar and maybe some mozzarella sticks from Big Mozz in the main concourse. Their sandwiches are also really tasty, but the sticks are notorious."

"Sounds nice."

After they ordered, Alan paid with cash and they waited at one of the tables until their mozzarella sticks and Alan's sandwich were ready. Eve had warned him that might be a lot of cheese, and he'd just laughed at her. "I'm from Holland, woman. We breathe cheese."

It didn't take them long, and Eve stood up to get their order. "Cheers!" she said, holding up her glass of cider.

He copied her gesture. "Cheers, gorgeous. So, what did you think of today's meeting?"

She put her glass back on the table. "Pretty much what you've been thinking. Nothing out of the ordinary. If the threat's coming from their side, he is blissfully unaware. Not undoable, I suppose, if the infiltration would have been set up years ago, but the way he explained the extra safety measures, I think it would be difficult enough for someone with enhanced abilities to do some serious damage, let alone for a 'normal' person, if you will."

Alan swirled the cider in his glass around. "Unless they are extremely enhanced like you or me."

She looked at him intently. "Is that something you picked up or just a random thought?"

He put the glass back down. "Just a random thought. Having said that, I know the Company specialises in people with enhanced abilities, but they can hardly be the only one. I'm sure the US has their version of the Company stashed away somewhere. Deep inside Area Fifty-One or God knows where. What?" Alan looked at Eve, who could barely suppress a laugh, he noticed.

"Area Fifty-One? I didn't think you were the conspiracy type, that's all."

He smiled. "Then I'll tell you what I tell my students at the beginning of each year. First lecture, we always delved deep into the mind. I used my powers, of course, to determine their emotions, so they would get slightly paranoid when I poked around in their minds and get all their feelings right. We would discuss interrogation techniques, and I'd even go as far to show them how you could make someone spill the beans, so to speak. I would end the lecture by saying 'So, always try to remember, just because you're paranoid, doesn't mean they're not after you. It might save your life one day.'" He felt a wave of content and curiosity.

"I wish I could have been in one of your classes. Sounds a whole lot better than the stuffy old professors I used to have. Seriously though, are you more of a Mulder or a Scully?"

He smiled. "Hmm, a bit of both, I think. I know too much. I feel too much. Oddly enough that's the science part of me. Underneath that all..." He gave her a wink. "I guess I want to believe."

"Well, I can honestly say, if there are aliens out there, I've never seen them at the Company. And I'm sure we would have loved to get our hands on one of them, but yes, I agree with you. England can't be the only country with a company such as mine. Are we going with that theory then?"

"No, I don't think so. I don't know about you, but somehow, this all feels mundane to me, for lack of a better word. I'm still going with terrorist attack."

She frowned. "That's not very soothing, you know. It widens the field far too much. Any country could be responsible. It could even be a lone gunman. Shall I text Roy to see if Leah has seen something more?"

"Not just yet. I still think we should hack into the system of the NYPD. Perhaps even the feds or the Pentagon."

"You want to hack into the Federal Bureau of Investigation? Or the bloody Pentagon? And pray tell, how exactly are you going to do that? Do you have some hidden talent I'm blissfully unaware of?"

He smiled. "No, but I know some people who could."

Eve frowned. "People you trust?"

"Not even remotely. He would screw us over big time, given the chance. However, he owes me and he knows it. He hates being in my debt. He will jump at the opportunity to have a clean slate, if you will. Plus, the Pentagon, any hacker would be interested. I do believe it's their Mount Everest. It certainly is for Marcello. The FBI will just be an added bonus."

"And you have the means to contact him?" she asked.

"If his number hasn't changed, I could give him a ring. Probably wise to send him a text first, though. He's a paranoid sucker and a call from an unknown number will definitely go straight to voicemail. That won't hurt, will it? From a burner phone, I mean?"

Eve looked at him. "That depends on how dodgy this guy is. If someone is keeping tabs on him, they can trace the text to this location. Mind you, I can't imagine that would mean much to anyone. We're at a very touristy place in the middle of New York City. I don't think it will raise any flags, so to speak."

"Dodgy is not the word I'd use for Marcello. Resourceful, perhaps. Annoying, most definitely. He managed to stay under the radar for many years. I can't say for sure, however, if this is still the case. I'll text him. I'll make sure it sounds harmless, but it'll mean something to him."

Eve moved closer to him so she could see what he was texting.

Gozer, tijd niet gesproken! Mount Everest al beklommen of ben je daar ondertussen te oud voor? Bel me als je die klim wilt doorstrepen van je bucket list. De Prof.

"Dutch, I presume?" Eve asked.

Alan nodded. "Yes. Basically, what I just texted is; *Dude, long time, no see. Did you manage to climb Mount Everest or are you getting too old for that? If you want to scratch that from your bucket list, call me. The Prof.*, short for professor, obviously. I considered signing with my own name, but he always calls me Professor, so I figured this would be better. What do you think? Press send?"

"Go for it. The sooner we know something, the better. I hate flying blind like this."

"That makes two of us." He hit send.

The phone rang within the minute. It showed no caller ID. "Well, here goes," Alan said.

Eve reached out to touch his hand. "If it's anybody else, hang up immediately. We'll ditch the phone and get out of here."

He nodded to convey he understood and pressed the green button to connect. "Hallo?" He said in Dutch and smiled at Eve and gave her a thumbs up to reassure her it was indeed Marcello. He continued the conversation in Dutch. "Ja, ik dacht al dat je dat interessant zou vinden…Gast, ik hou je niet voor de gek. Ik heb je echt hiervoor nodig en jij bent degene die zei dat geen berg te hoog was, als je begrijpt wat ik bedoel. En voor mijn part pak je ze allebei en doe je de K2 er meteen achteraan joh, makkie voor jou!" He remained silent for a while to listen what Marcello had to say.

"Het interesseert me geen reet wat voor 'spul' je nodig hebt, man, zet het maar op mijn rekening. Maar ik verwacht dan wel een soort van nieuw wereldrecord, Marcello, gaat dat lukken?…Nee, ik ben momenteel in de Big Apple, ik wil absoluut die ball drop een keer meemaken, schijnt nogal spectaculair te zijn. Explosief zelfs als je de kranten moet geloven met al die lichtgevende kristallen… Ja joh, je moet er al in de middag zijn, duizenden en duizenden mensen die speciaal hiervoor komen…Nee, niet bepaald mijn ding, maar ik vond het tijd om eens wat anders te proberen, zou jou ook goed doen." He was quiet again.

"Marcello, ik kan eerlijk zeggen dat als jij dit voor elkaar krijgt, je wat mij betreft met pensioen kan en de rest van je leven met je pik kan spelen. Hebben we een deal?" He listened again. "Midden in de nacht werkt voor mij…Nee, ik bel jou. Oh, en Marcello? Klim niet zonder touw heh." Alan disconnected.

"Okay, so I could pick up what you were thinking, but besides 'hallo' I didn't understand a single word. Translation, please." Eve scooted closer to him.

He smiled. "Well, all things considered, that actually went pretty well. Mind you, it's going to cost us. He needs, or claims he needs, a lot of expensive equipment for this."

Eve shrugged. "Don't care. This credit card is pretty much limitless and cannot be traced back to me or the Company, so even if he spends a million, I wouldn't blink twice. Somewhere in there I caught the words 'Big Apple' and 'ball drop', or did my ears deceive me?"

"No, you heard correctly. Marcello and I always have a certain build-up in a conversation. Like I said, he's pretty paranoid. So, I always begin with the organisation I want hacked. In this case, the Pentagon. Which is why I mentioned Mount Everest. He'll know how to translate that."

"How will he know to look into the FBI as well?" Eve asked.

"Well, he won't, but Marcello's very thorough. Which is why I mentioned he could kill two birds with one stone and climb the K2 as well. It's the second highest mountain in the world. Unfortunately, this is the only part that leaves too much room for interpretation. The second part of our conversation is the target. Which is why I mentioned I'm currently enjoying my stay in the Big Apple because the ball drop is supposed to be spectacular. Even explosive with all those radiant crystals. My way of letting him know what he's supposed to be looking for. Any intel on the ball drop. Of course, he could interpret K2 as the CIA or NSA instead of the FBI, but does it really matter? Marcello always delivers. If there's something to be found, he will find it. I also let him off the hook if he pulls this off. So, he knows I'll never bother him again once he delivers. He liked that. Very much, I could tell through the phone."

"You can pick up his emotions through the phone?" Eve asked.

"Can't you?" he returned.

Eve frowned. "Well, yes, but those are words. In thought, I'll grant you that, but they're still words. I didn't realise it worked the same way with emotions."

"Why? Because Tristan couldn't?" he asked, his voice dripping with sarcasm.

"That's not nice, Alan, but yes. Did you know or guess?"

He shrugged. "It was a guess, but it doesn't surprise me. Tristan, I'm sure, is the kind of man who doesn't want to use his powers unless absolutely necessary or when he thinks he's doing the right thing. Trust me, he could if he wanted to. Probably even from a greater distance than I can."

She looked bothered. "He's not some kind of angel, you know. Tristan had done plenty of things he's not very proud of."

"Ah, but my darling, that's my point exactly. He feels guilty about those things. I do not. Well, maybe one or two things, but other than that, shit happens. And with it, some collateral damage. My parents never asked to be hurt. They are good people, and shit happened to them, anyway. I learned the hard way life isn't fair. It's not judgemental. You don't get a cookie if you try your hardest. Sometimes, things just go your way and sometimes, they don't. It's as simple as that. Why live with all the guilt? It's soul consuming, a waste of life. Am I scaring you?" he asked when he noticed she was looking at him intently.

"No. And for future reference, I don't scare easily. At first, I thought you sounded a bit bitter. Tainted by your past, perhaps, but this really is your outlook on life, isn't it? I think I have a slightly more positive outlook on life, but I do understand what you're saying. I never believed that God, or the universe, awarded or punished your efforts or lack thereof, either. We are responsible for our own choices, but we do have a tendency to look for that cookie if we really do our best, don't we?" She gave him a soft smile.

He emptied the last of his cider. "Yes, we do. Although, I have to admit, I have been wondering what I've done right to deserve someone like you." He took her hand and pressed his lips against it. As gently as he'd taken her hand, he dropped it on the table and almost choked to death.

"Alan? Alan, what's wrong, are you okay?" Eve frantically whispered to him, reaching out to hold him upright.

"I can't feel Kate anymore. She's gone!" he managed to choke out.

"Gone? What do you mean, gone? Is she dead?"

He looked into her eyes. "No. I've never felt anything like this. She's not 'here' anymore. She's not on this Earth."

Eve was about to say something, when the burner phone in her pocket started to vibrate.

Catherine

She felt strange. There was somewhere she needed to be, if only her eyes would open. Her body felt heavy, like it was being weighed down. What was the last thing she remembered? Ah yes, the cake. Did she fall on it? Was she unconscious? No, she was pretty sure the texture beneath her hands felt different to that in her guest room. It almost felt like dirt. Soft dirt, like she was lying in a field. A cornfield. Suddenly everything moved in fast forward. The painting! Her breathing accelerated.

Stay calm. Stay calm, she chanted to herself. *Okay, so you're inside a freaking painting, so what? If you can get in, there has to be a way out as well.*

Yes, that was a comforting thought. She was going to hold onto that one. Now to determine if she was in any immediate danger. Carefully she honed her elements within close proximity. There was something there. A presence, it felt human. Not too near, but watching her nonetheless. It felt harmless, though. Caring even, like the presence was checking to see if she was okay. It slowly came closer towards her and she tensed her muscles just in case her powers were off.

"Catherine? Are you okay, honey? I need you to turn around and open your eyes. Are you in any pain?"

Catherine froze to the ground. She knew that voice. A voice she had last heard when she was a little girl. Suddenly, she was that little girl again, playing with her My Little Pony and galloping with it down the stairs. Too fast and she and her pony went tumbling down. Her grandmother had been looking after her because her mom and dad had been at work. Those exact words. *"Catherine? Are you okay, honey? I*

need you to turn around and open your eyes. Are you in any pain?"
Impossible. It couldn't be. Her mind was playing tricks on her.
Her grandmother was dead. Maybe the painting was some sort
of dreamscape and it had manifested her grandmother because
Catherine missed her. Yes, that made much more sense.

She heard the voice again.

"Catherine? You're okay, honey. Don't be scared. I just want to
talk to you," her grandmother's voice said.

*Well, of course, I'm okay. Possibly going bonkers, perhaps, hearing the
dead and all, but sooner or later everybody goes to the zoo. Otherwise
I feel fine.* And she did. She flexed her fingers and wiggled her toes.
Nothing. No pain, no strange sensation of something being wrong
with her body. With a deep breath, she pushed herself up and rolled
over on her back to sit up straight. A woman was staring at her with
a concerned look. Flaming red hair, green eyes like hers, exactly
the same as Catherine remembered her. She hadn't aged a day.
Definitely a dream then.

"Hello, Nana. It's good to see you."

The woman's concerned look turned into a frown. "I see this will
take some convincing. You think this isn't real," she said.

Catherine stood up. "How can it be? I don't want to be
inconsiderate here, but you've been dead for most of my life. And
unless Eve is way more powerful than I give her credit for, I'm
pretty sure even she cannot raise the dead after decades of no brain
activity. Not to mention there would be nothing left to revive."
There, that sounded reasonable. Logical even.

Her grandmother smiled. "She did, however, successfully revive
you when the blast of the asteroid killed you."

Catherine smiled as well. "Ah yes, she did. But you could have
picked that from my memory. Tristan told me everything this
afternoon, so it's fresh at the surface."

"So, this is all happening in your mind?" she asked. "Okay, so
let's go with that theory. Then I would only be privy to your mind.

Your memories, wouldn't you agree?"

Catherine thought about that and slowly nodded her consent. "I suppose that sounds about right."

"Will you walk with me? I will tell you the story of this painting we're in and how it came into my possession."

"Sure," Catherine agreed and they both moved slowly through the cornfield.

"I always knew that one day I would have to tell you the truth and just showing up on your doorstep seemed a bit, dramatic, even to my taste. Besides, with your powers, one can never be sure what damage you would have done. So, I needed a safe haven. Somewhere where I could explain why I did what I did and you would not hurt yourself. Or anyone else, for that matter. It took me many years to track down this painting. It is one of a kind. Well, I say one of a kind, there are actually two. Twins, you see. Together they create a portal. The artist never knew it's potential, that came later. By a group of people with tremendous power, but I won't get into that now. They almost ruined everything, but I managed to get rid of them. You see, Tristan was close to uncovering the truth about these paintings and I couldn't have that. So, I had Alan retrieve that information before he could read it. You can verify this later with Tristan, if you please. It is of little consequence to the story, though." She looked sideways to see if her granddaughter was still listening.

"Please, continue," Catherine said, though she didn't like the sound of how her grandmother had used the phrase "get rid of them".

"I've always wanted you to have a normal childhood. To get to experience life. And you have. Just look at you. You've become an amazing woman. I'm extremely proud of you."

Catherine blushed. "You don't have to say that, Nana. I know you are proud of me. I've always felt loved by you, by my family." Her grandmother looked sad.

"I'm glad you grew up feeling loved. And you're right. I did love you. I still do. So, I did everything in my power to keep you safe. Of course, I failed. On several occasions. You know I'm a seer. Like you're friend Leah. She has a lot of potential. My powers are a bit more developed, though. I knew your future. I saw your death and I did everything in my power to steer you away from it. Every decision I made, every road I took, it always ended the same. The asteroid, you saving the Earth, at your own expense. It would not do. I started looking for other gifted people. After all, we could not be the only ones. And then, I found her. Just a young girl, but, Catherine, I wish you could have seen it. The power, the potential. To actually restart life, I'd never seen anything like it."

"Eve," I mumbled.

She nodded. "Yes, Eve. My little reviver."

A chill ran across Catherine's body as she spoke those words, but her grandmother didn't seem to notice or chose to ignore it.

"Suddenly, it was all very clear. I saw a new future. A future where you would live, but I could not be a part of that future. I had to take myself out of the equation. You could never know if you even stood a chance of surviving. The confrontation with Alan, the transferral of his power of death to your body. There were some hiccups along the way. In the end, Tristan falling in love with you, it was the only scenario that ended to my satisfaction. You being alive. And yes, I did everything in my power to achieve that outcome. I'm not sorry for the things I've done, Catherine. I would do them again. I am sorry I could not protect you. Sorry you had to lose your father. If I could have stepped in without changing the outcome of your future, I would have, my child."

Catherine's mind was struggling, trying to make sense of the words her grandmother was saying. It had to be a dream. Or more accurately, some kind of nightmare. Intensified by this blasted painting. The painting. She'd said there were two.

"Where is the other painting?" Catherine asked her.

The older woman stopped. "In my office. It's also where I've been living for the past thirty years. You would know it as the Company."

"No." Catherine shook her head. "That's ridiculous. Uncle Ben went to the morgue, he recognised you. You were wearing this ring." She pointed to the ring on her finger.

"My dear girl, he saw what we wanted him to see. Your mother and Ben were filled with grief. I died in a plane crash, remember. Of course, he recognised the ring. We had planted it there on the poor woman's finger. She only had to resemble my height and posture, there wasn't much else to go by. You know how easy it is to change dental records and DNA when you have gifted people working for you?"

"What exactly are you saying? You rule the Company? You're the Serpent? Yes, Tristan told me that cute little name they have for his boss. Or, at least, the big boss, not his direct boss. I'm pretty sure that's a man. We sent him a letter."

"Yes, that was very sweet of you. Trevor showed it to me. For a minute, I was afraid Tristan would disobey me again and tell you all about his latest discovery."

"Now I know you're lying. Tristan would never do that. He promised he would never lie to me again after the asteroid incident." Her grandmother, who she still wasn't sure was real, laughed.

"Oh, my darling. Of course, he would. All I had to convince him of was that it was imperative to your survival that I'd tell you all this myself. Tristan would do many things, Catherine, but he would never endanger your life. Like you said, not after the asteroid incident. The poor man is in love with you, after all. Love makes fools of us all. I'm glad to see he took my warning seriously. I have trouble with seeing the immediate future, you see? I never used to, but old age is finally catching up with me, I suppose. Don't you agree it's much better to hear this from me than it would be from him? You're having a hard time as it is believing it from my mouth, let alone his. You would think he'd gone crazy."

Catherine tried to look at this logically. "Why now? Why not keep this a secret forever? Yes, I've mourned you, but it was many years ago. The wounds have healed, and Mom and I and Uncle Ben, we've found a way to move on. So, why now?"

She nodded. "That is a good question. I started my story saying I wanted you to have a normal childhood, to grow up and live your life. From the moment I saw the asteroid, it became about finding a way to preserve your life. But you're grown up now and, if I might add, alive and kicking. Danger is always lurking around the corner, and I'm running out of time. You see, Catherine, it has always been my intention for you to take over. Someone capable has to run the Company and that someone has always been you. How could there be another choice? I briefly considered my own daughter, but Elizabeth doesn't have what it takes to run this company. My Company. She's too gentle, if you will. Not that your heart isn't in the right place, Catherine, but I'm sure you'll agree this position is not for the faint hearted. I've done many things for the greater good. Yes, I know you hate that phrase. But ask yourself, you were willing to sacrifice your own life for the greater good, weren't you? Can you honestly look me in the eye and tell me there's was no doubt in your mind you would survive the asteroid?" She looked at Catherine.

"Of course, I wasn't sure!" she heatedly replied. "However, I do think that's something other than toying with other people's lives. And I refuse to believe my grandmother would ever do such a thing."

"Please, Catherine, spare me the drama. You'd be surprised what I'm capable of. Or you yourself, for that matter. Or have you forgotten how you almost destroyed Alan?"

Catherine's breath hitched. That hurt. "That's not the same. He was going to hurt me. It was self-defence."

"Ah yes, but he wasn't going to hurt you, now was he? One of my minor mistakes, you see. I never saw you attacking him.

From that moment, you had the power of death. Alan could have trained you, prepared you for what was to come, but you decided to destroy him. At least, that was the original plan, having Alan train with you. With Alan out of the picture, I had to change plans because you remained blissfully unaware of the fact you had his powers."

"It was a split decision," Catherine mumbled. "I never meant to hurt him."

Her grandmother looked at her and sighed. "Maybe. Maybe not. I'm not here to judge you, Catherine. I know sometimes you have to make choices you do not like. It is part of taking responsibility for your actions. And besides, matters little now. What's done is done. I put a lot of energy in a program that would be able to bring Alan back. Eve would be able to revive him, obviously, but I needed his mind intact as well. You see, I wasn't sure you would fall for Tristan. It was my one variable. Love is always very tricky when it comes to seeing the future. You would have believed Alan. Probably would have scared the living daylights out of you, but you would have believed him. One way or another, you would know you could do this. I almost blew my own cover when I got Trevor's report you were planning on invoking some goddess to destroy the asteroid. Really, my child, what were you thinking?"

"Yes, well excuse me for being in a bit of panic mode during that time, Grandmother," Catherine replied, her voice dripping with sarcasm. "Next time, I'll be sure to rely on my own powers."

The Serpent smiled. "You're cross with me. I can tell by the way you said grandmother. You always call me Nana. No, it's okay. Don't apologise. Like I said, I'm not sorry for what I've done, and I would do it all again, but I do have a lot to apologise for. I would be angry, too. Do you still believe this is a dream?"

Catherine hesitated. It certainly was so completely out there. How could it be real? Then again, it felt awfully real. From her own experience, the things she usually wasn't very happy about, turned out to be the real deal. She looked so young though, just the way she remembered her. "You haven't aged one bit. Most people would consider that a sign that this can only be a figment of my own imagination."

The older woman smiled. "Then you have to take a closer look, Catherine. I have aged, though perhaps not in the normal, human way. You look very young for a thirty-six-year-old woman. We elementals age quite gracefully. It's the element of fire, you see. It's rejuvenating. Well, if you know how to use it. Look into my eyes, though and tell me what you see."

Her grandmother stood perfectly still. Catherine hesitated just a few seconds but decided she would have to take a chance. If this was a dream, nothing bad could happen to her. If it really was her grandmother, well, she had just pretty much confessed to have gone out of her way to keep her alive this far, why hurt her now? Catherine took a step closer and looked into her eyes. Catherine's own eyes. It was a bit unsettling. She let all her elements come to the surface and then she felt it. The pain, the heartache, the dedication, the love. There were also darker emotions and even a touch of doubt. She hadn't always been this sure about everything. This was her grandmother, though. She felt exactly the same as the woman who had braided her hair when she was a little girl. She could feel her eyes tearing up. Her grandmother's eyes looked awfully bright as well.

"Nana?" she asked before she closed the space between them and put her arms around her grandmother. She really was crying, barely aware her grandmother soothingly stroked her back, telling her it was going to be all right. Slowly she pulled back to look at her grandmother.

"Sorry, I've been a bit emotional the last couple of months." She wiped the tears from her eyes. Her grandmother gave her a soft smile.

"I think that is only to be expected with what you have gone through, sweetheart. Not to mention this little bombshell I've just dropped on you."

Catherine took a deep breath. "I don't care. I can't believe you're still alive. Mom is going to be so happy!" She stopped when she noticed the sad look on her grandmother's face. "You don't want her to know." It wasn't a question.

"I'm so sorry, my child. I know this is a terrible burden I'm putting on your shoulders, but your mother cannot know. Like you said, she has moved on now. That is a good thing. She cannot know, Catherine. It will put her in danger. Make her a target even. Would you risk losing your mother as well?"

"What? No, of course not. But, Nana, what is it that you're asking of me, exactly? I can't tell anyone? How the hell am I supposed to keep this a secret? Leah's a seer herself, for God's sake!"

"Come, walk with me to the other side." They moved towards the end of the field. It became blurry around the edges. "There on the other side is my office. That world will soon become yours. I wish I could give you more time, my dear, I really do."

Catherine squinted her eyes to see the outlines of an office somewhere outside the painting. Out there was the Company. Her grandmother's company. Tristan's company. Tristan. "He knows! Tristan knows, I can talk about this to him, right? Wait, hang on, what do mean you wish you could give me more time? You said something like that before. Are you dying? Are you sick?" She reached out to her elements. She didn't feel sick. She felt healthy.

"Like I said, we elementals age a little bit differently. No, I'm not sick, but I'm no spring chicken, Catherine dear. I would like to know I leave this world in capable hands, and I want to be prepared for that. Is that so very wrong of me?"

Catherine shrugged. "I suppose not. What if I don't like your company, Nana. I mean, I know you're a great seer, so I guess you know that better than I do, but from what I've heard from Tristan—which is very little, by the way—it doesn't really sound like my cup of tea. I like my life. I like Elements. I don't want to give that up."

"Who says you will have to? The Company pretty much runs itself, Catherine. Well, that's not entirely true and we did have some setbacks this year, but I'm hoping that will all play out exactly as I'm hoping it will turn out. The important thing right now is to get your story straight. Our time here is almost up. Once the painting starts to vibrate, you will have to be on the other side to return to your home."

Catherine rubbed her temples. "Oh my God. Nana, everyone's there. Mom's there, Simon, Uncle Ben, Lee, Deb, Tristan, all my friends. How am I ever going to pull this off? I can't do this, Nana. I just can't."

"Yes, you can. You are my granddaughter and you were always meant for something greater. You're much stronger than you give yourself credit for. And if I may give you a word of advice, loss of memory. When anyone asks where you have been or what you've seen, just say you can't remember. That it was all very blurry."

"Lie to them, you mean? Lovely! Because I've always been such a good liar. Christ, Nana, I can't keep a secret to safe my own life, let alone somebody else! I really think you picked the wrong person."

Her grandmother shook her head. "I have not. Now pull yourself together, we don't have much time. Focus on Tristan. You won't have to hide anything from him. I will need to see you before you fly out tomorrow afternoon. He will bring you to me. You will bring Leah and Deborah with you."

"What? But you just said I couldn't tell anyone."

"And you can't. Yet, they will accompany you. I'm seeing it very clearly now. Hmm, yes. Leah knows more about the ball drop. Tristan will advise to work together on this and bring you to the Company. Leah and Deborah will refuse to let you go alone." Her eyes became focussed again and she looked at Catherine. "Are you ready? Can you do this for me?"

Catherine felt a full-blown panic attack coming on. "No! Nana, no. This is my life! My choice!"

Her grandmother grabbed her shoulders and shook her gently. "Catherine! Snap out of it. Look, it's very simple, plausible deniability. Do you want to endanger your family and friends? Those you hold dear? No. Of course, you don't. I didn't, either. That's why I know you can do this. My blood is running through your veins. Keep them safe. Focus on Tristan. Come see me in the morning. You can do this. Now, you have to move." The painting was starting to vibrate.

"Come on, hurry." Her grandmother all but dragged her to the beginning of the cornfield, where she had entered the painting.

"What about you? Don't you have to get out on the other side?"

"Don't worry about me. I can look after myself. Remember, I love you, but most of all, I believe in you."

She gave her a great push and Catherine felt herself falling backwards, like she was being pulled down by the undertow in a whirling sea.

Eve

They were back at the hotel. Both Eve and Alan had been doing everything they could possibly think of to find a way to get Catherine out of a bloody painting. Eve had seen a lot of weird shit in her life, but people being absorbed by a painting hadn't been one of them. She would have had a hard time believing it, if it wasn't that she heard it from Roy himself. Tristan said he'd had examined the painting, even shook it up and down, but nothing had changed. They had looked for her inside the painting, with a magnifying glass but came up empty. No one was inside the painting. At least, not to the naked eye. Eve knew Tristan had considered taking it off the wall and keeping it at the Company. He'd decided against it because he had a pretty good guess who had triggered the painting. Privately, Eve agreed with him. This had the Serpent written all over it. And then they would have to assume Catherine would find a way back to their world.

Alan was walking around the room like a caged lion. He'd never felt anything like it. "I can't believe she could be this stupid! Leave it to Kate to go hug a bloody occult painting on the exact moment of her birth!"

"I hardly think she actually hugged it, love. She was probably drawn to it for a reason. If anything, the Serpent is very thorough. And the painting has a strange pull to begin with. You of all people should know that. You have touched it. Dreamed about it, even."

He waved a hand in the air, dismissing her comments. "Yes, yes, I know all that. All the more reason for her to stay the fuck away from it. Have you found anything else on the dark web?"

Eve turned back to her laptop. "Nothing we didn't already know. Painter Carlos Vargas painted it in the late eighteen hundreds.

Sacred Valley of the Incas, also known as *Urubamba Valley*, was first procured by the Museo Inka, after the painter's death. It remained there for quite some time, until it found its way to Europe. Was sold to the Louvre after the first world war and remained there till the early fifties. Then it found its way to the Met, where it stayed until it went back to Europe on loan for the Peruvian Exhibition at the National Gallery in London. Well, we pretty much know the inside story from there on, don't we?"

"Mm, yes," Alan agreed. "Nothing else?"

"Well, it says here the Church of Scientology expressed an interest in the painting in 1953 before it went to Europe. Apparently, they were outbid by the Louvre because obviously the painting ended up in Paris. They have shown a great deal of interest in many pieces of art, though, so I don't know whether or not it's noteworthy. Hang on, here's something that might be of interest. Museo Inka reported the painting stolen in 1827. They got it back anonymously three years later, in 1830. It says here they never found out who took the painting. Well, that isn't mentioned anywhere on Google. Believe me, I tried."

Alan started to walk around the room again. "Okay, so here's my theory. I don't think the painter had anything to do with the painting's 'hidden talents', if you will. He claimed the Incas were his ancestors. Whether or not this is true is not really important, I think. And, he was obviously a very good painter. The details of the corn alone are truly magnificent. The painting feels alive, like you could step right into that field. The painter's good, but that feeling can't be all due to the artist's skill. Shame he never got to profit from it. I just saw what the Louvre had to lay down for that cornfield. That is a lot of money."

"It is. What makes it quite interesting is there aren't a lot of paintings. Tapestries, yes, but almost no paintings. Most of it are sculptures or pottery. Lots of gold artefacts, obviously. They had an obsession with gold. And even though this is not from the

Incan period, the artist did have a claim to their ancestry. It probably increased its value."

Alan nodded. "I agree. I think the occult part came during the period it was stolen. There are plenty of powerful organisations who dabble in the occult. I've run across several when I was touring the world, giving lectures."

"Not so many with the power and means to pull off something like this, though." Eve remarked.

"True. But how many organisations do you know who could invent a project like Dreamcatcher, successfully revive a man after many, many years, brain capacity fully intact?"

"One," Eve replied, narrowing her eyes. "You mean to imply the Company had something to do with this?"

Alan shook his head. "No. you mistake my meaning. Besides, they weren't around when the painting's powers were invoked, created or whatever. No, but I do think the Company has the power and means to track down such valuable items and claim them as their own. Also, I think Dreamcatcher is the reason I had a vision about this very painting, even before I was assigned to this mission. I think the Serpent planted it there, in my mind. Because I know you most certainly didn't do that. And because Kate and I still have a connection on some level. She dreamt the same dream. Only seen from her perspective."

"We've had a lot of trial and error with Dreamcatcher," Eve mused. "They terminated the program the moment you escaped from the Company. Weird, come to think of it, as it was basically on her orders you did escape. She let you escape. To get the painting."

"Yes, she did. Or, back then, when I still believed I was dealing with a him. I did not know the Company's Serpent was no one other than Catherine's grandmother. I have to believe she wanted me to get it safely into her apartment because she could not foresee a better way of letting her granddaughter know she's still alive. I think she preserved a memory of her own inside that painting. One that has been triggered by Kate turning thirty-six."

"What exactly are you saying? That they're both inside the painting right now? Don't you think that's a bit far-fetched? Why not invite her over to the Company? Why go to all this trouble for a tête-a-tête with her granddaughter? I'll give you one thing, I agree with you this whole painting business has the Serpent written all over it. But still, just for a simple conversation?"

"You said it yourself. At the Company, someone is always listening. And she might have reasons of her own. Maybe she's seen that Tristan will tell her the truth, maybe she's dying, I don't know."

"You don't think, though. Do you?"

"No. It doesn't add up. Something like this would have taken a great deal of precise timing, a great deal of effort has gone in to this. With her abilities, she would have seen Tristan,—or anyone else for that matter—coming a mile away. I would like to point out one thing. Nothing, and I do mean nothing, will be 'simple' when Kate finds out her grandmother is still alive. If I'm right though, Kate will find a way back to our world and hopefully, soon. If I'm wrong, well…" He didn't finish his sentence.

"Right. Well, let's not go there. Should I inform Roy about our theory?"

Alan nodded once. "Yes, I think you should. It might calm Tristan's nerves just a bit. At the very least, it will give him something to focus on."

Eve smiled. "I didn't know you cared."

"I do not. Not about him, that is. I admire his abilities, yes, but he is not exactly a favourite of mine. He is one of yours though, and Kate loves him. Besides, he let us go, I owe him for that. So, like I said, the least I can do is ease his mind when possible."

"I'll call him right now," Eve said to him, picking up her phone. "Roy, it's me. Any news?…Still inside the painting then? Bugger…

No, not much. We did find some interesting titbits on the dark web, and Alan came up with a theory with sounds plausible to the both of us." She was quiet for a moment. "Okay, hold on, I'll ask." Eve held the phone out to Alan. "He would like to talk to you himself. Do you mind?"

Alan held out his hand in reply. She gave the phone to him and walked over to the minibar. She could use a drink. She held up a small bottle of red wine, and Alan nodded his head in approval. So far Alan voice remained calm and his tone was polite. She couldn't hear Roy's response, but she could hear Alan's thoughts. Tristan was having a seriously bad day. She figured as much. Tristan was the protective type all the way. He would see this as his personal failure. She put the glass down on the partner desk for Alan and went to sit on the couch with her own glass and raised it in salute to Alan. He gave her a smile.

While Alan's mind was focussed on the conversation with Roy, Eve took her chance to examine him carefully. She seldom got the chance as he immediately caught her looking at him and picked up on her emotions. She wondered about that. Tristan had left her to her own devices most of the time. Having heard Alan's statement that Tristan's empathic abilities outshone his own, Eve looked back on their relationship in a different way. She'd always known Tristan was a gentleman. Especially when Charles had taken him under his wing. Dear Charles. Manners were so important to him.

"*It's what separates the men from the boys, Eve. You would do well to remember that,*" he'd said to her once. And she had taken that to heart.

Of course, most men and women ran a mile once they found out what she could do. People didn't like having their minds invaded. Tristan had been different. He had actually sought her out once he found out what she could do. At first, she had thought he'd just been interested in her abilities, but reading his mind showed her he was really interested in her, not just her abilities and had nothing to do with personal gain or him trying to use her. They had learned a lot from each other. He had been her rock. Being a mind reader and a reviver meant leading a pretty lonely life. Eve never had a lot of friends. Most of her teens were spent at the Company. She had been recruited at a very young age. Her own parents had been quite scared of her and were only too happy to place her in a "school" for gifted students. And Eve had been taught. She'd had the best tutors the Company's money could buy, but she was seldom allowed to play with children her own age. Not that there were many at the Company. Her parents never came to visit her. They had always sent her a birthday present and a Christmas card. She got to spend a couple of weeks during summer at home. After four years, Eve stopped calling it home. When she turned sixteen, she told her parents she was going to see Europe with some friends. They didn't even bother to protest or ask whether she would be safe. She'd never spoken to them since. The Company had been her family, but even there, she was the outsider. The one everyone feared.

Tristan did not only encourage her to mingle with her co-workers, he had brought Charles and Roy into her life. Of course, she knew Charles had warned him about her. Eve had built up quite the reputation and she guessed she proved him right in the end. She had ended up hurting Tristan. Eve sighed and took another sip of her wine. Alan was still talking to Roy. She heard the words Pentagon and hacker, so she assumed Alan was filling him in on that as well. He was being remarkably open. She wondered if the Serpent had foreseen this. Her ending up with Alan. Catherine, or Kate, with Tristan. What were the odds? At first, she had been jealous as hell. Tristan loving another woman didn't sit well with her at all. In all fairness, she had been fascinated by Alan from the start. He would never apologise for being powerful. She liked that.

When Alan escaped from the Company, ending up on her doorstep, she'd been a little more than surprised. She was intrigued. Alan had told her she had been the logical choice, from a psychological perspective. Eve had worked with him almost every day once she had revived him. Serpent's orders. Probably because she was able to read his mind and he would feel obliged to her because she basically had saved his life. He had been fascinated by her abilities and vice versa. One could say they had formed a connection. Reading his mind that night on her doorstep, she'd decided to invite him inside. And she had learned a lot from him that night. There had been no doubt in her mind he told her the truth. She knew an empath could have manipulated her mind, but she was absolutely positive he had not used his powers on her. That was the first time she had started to see him in a different light. Eve hadn't been lying when she'd told Tristan she was tired of being alone. Alan had kissed her when he'd left her apartment. She could still remember that kiss.

She drained the last of her wine and noticed Alan was coming to an end with his conversation with Roy. He motioned to her if she wanted her phone back, and she shrugged. Alan held it out to her, though, so she got up anyway.

"Hey, Roy, anything you can work with?"

"Okay, I take it back. You might not be a total idiot."

Eve snorted. "Thanks so much, Roy. Pray tell, on what account?"

"Alan gave me useful information. He will fill you in on the whole ball drop thing. I got some pretty interesting information as well from Leah."

She frowned. "Where exactly are you, Roy?" He had been speaking quietly, not raising his voice, like she was used to whenever he was on edge or annoyed.

"In Kate's apartment. We were invited to her birthday party, so we were here when it happened. Needless to say, I can't get Tristan to move so much as one inch away from the stupid painting, so I guided both Leah and Kate's mom from the room. I'm sure Alan will tell you everything. Look, Eve, I don't know how she's coming out of this. Leah is thinking of cancelling their New York trip. I've talked her out of it so far, telling her to wait and see what Kate says. You still have the other burner phone?"

"Yes," she confirmed.

"Good, get rid of this one, Eve. You've used it too many times already. I'm good, but I'm not that good."

Eve smiled. "Will do right after your call, Roy. You will keep us posted, right?"

"As soon as I have anything worthwhile to share, Eve. That goes for you guys as well, though. And stay safe!" He disconnected.

* * *

They had arrived at 1501 Broadway, home of the Bubba Gump Shrimp Company. Eve had chosen it because they both liked shrimp, the service was good, but most of all, it was always crowded and a bit noisy. Nobody would be paying attention to their conversation, and that was what they needed right now.

Eve had given the burner phone to a homeless person on the street. Alan had asked her why she didn't just dump the phone.

Eve had shaken her head. "No, this way the phone will still be moving around, at least for as long as the battery is charged. If someone is tracking us, at least we'll give them something to track. Besides, did you see the look on his face? I just made his day!"

He had rolled his eyes and had kissed the top of her head.

"Hello, folks. How are we today? My name is Danny, and I'll be your server for tonight. Here's some water for you guys. Are we ready for drinks?"

Eve gave him a dazzling smile. "I think so. I would like the Rum Forrest Rum." She saw Alan bite back a laugh.

"Well, if we're going exotic, I'm going for the Classic Coronarita." She stared at him.

Danny handed them the menu. "Excellent choices, if I may say so. I'll be right back with your drinks."

Eve put the menu down. "Seriously? The Coronarita?"

Alan grinned. "Why not? I always liked the beer, and I just

made a deal with a guy who's an absolute master in planting viruses and probably hacking into the Pentagon as we speak. Call me crazy, but I thought it sounded like an appropriate drink."

She just shook her head, mumbling something about men. Danny was back with their drinks. They were both humongous.

"Here we go, folks. Are you ready to order or do we need another minute?"

"Another minute, please. I'm sorry, I haven't even looked at the menu."

"Not at all, sir. Just give me a wave whenever you're ready." Danny left their table.

"Nice guy," Alan commented.

Eve nodded. "They're known for their service. I've been here before. Your drink comes with the glass, by the way. They will give you a new one down in the store."

"Really?" Alan looked at his glass more carefully and saw the Bubba Gump logo on it. "Well, that's nice. Good marketing, too."

"Do you see anything you like?" Eve asked.

Alan looked at her. "Absolutely. I assume you mean on the menu, though?"

She felt her cheeks go red. "Yes, Alan. The menu." She stuck out her tongue. He reached for her hand across the table and gave it a soft squeeze.

"I mean it, though. There's no one else I'd rather be on the run with." He gave her a wink, but his voice sounded serious.

"I can think of worse company as well," she replied.

"Nice choice of words," he said with a grin. Eve rolled her eyes.

"Oh, har har. Just pick something of the damn menu. I'm starving. What is it with this city? I'm always hungry here."

Alan nodded. "It's all the walking around. I've noticed it, too. You take the Underground more often in London. Here, you do use it to get across town, but you still walk several blocks. Probably because there's so much to see."

"Perhaps. London has many gems as well, though. I like London."
He smiled. "I know you do. Me, I think I could get used to this city. I like the vibe. Funny, I've been to many places in the world. Somehow, New York never made the list. I've been to the States several times, just never on this side."

"Where have you been?" Eve asked. She was really curious. There was still so much about Alan she didn't know. They were just getting to know one another a little better.

"Let's pick something first before poor Danny comes back and we still haven't decided."

She smiled. "Okay, I've decided. I love their Clam Chowder, and I'm just going to ask for two skewers of grilled shrimp on the side."

"Do you think that'll be enough?" he asked.

"Yes, they also have a bowl, you see?" She pointed to the cup and larger bowl option on the menu.

"Oh, right. Well, I'm going for the Shrimpers' Heaven. Sounds like it will live up to its name."

Danny was keeping an eye out for them and came over immediately when Alan gave him a wave. He asked if Eve would like the skewers and soup served separately or all together.

"All together, please." She gave him another smile before he left to help another table. "So, tell me, which parts of the States have you seen?" she asked.

"My first time was Los Angeles, actually. It was for a lecture. I was not a fan. Don't know why, exactly. Something off with the vibe. I never quite got why they call it the City of Angels. I didn't feel that. Santa Monica, at the beach, was okay. I found myself driving there almost every night. More relaxed, more artistic, I think. I had a few days after the seminar, though and drove up to San Francisco. Loved that city! Have you ever been?"

Eve shook her head. "No, I've actually only ever been on this side of the States. I've heard a lot of good things about San Francisco, though. Who knows, someday. Did you visit any other parts?"

He nodded. "Yes. Because San Francisco agreed with me so much, I went back for a holiday and toured California, Nevada, Utah and Arizona by car. You know, Yosemite, Bryce Canyon, Grand Canyon, Death Valley, Vegas, because, why not?" He grinned.

"Haha, did you win anything?"

He looked pretty smug. "Actually, I did. Probably beginner's luck, though. I never tried again. But let's just say the holiday didn't cost me a thing."

"Wow! You must have won big."

"It was quite stupid, to be honest. I had a few too many to drink and decided to put everything on black. Lucky for me, it turned out in my favour. Winning that much money sobered me up like nothing else, so I had the presence of mind to take my winnings and get the hell out of there before I could be tempted to give it another go."

"Very wise. You know what they say, the house always wins."

"I also went to the deep south a couple of times. Louisiana, Mississippi, Alabama, Georgia. Love the music, love the kitchen, love the people. I have a soft spot for New Orleans. First time I stepped into a bar these guys were playing jazz. But it wasn't just the band. Some of the locals just joined in. The band didn't seem to mind, like this was business as usual. I kept coming back after that night. On the third night, I was brave enough to bring along my saxophone—"

"You play the saxophone?" Eve interrupted him.

"I suppose there's a lot we don't know about each other. But yes, I played for more than twenty years. My father used to be in a blues band. Not professionally, just for fun, but he did tour in the Netherlands. Just local pubs and stuff. When I was a teenager, I could come along if I behaved myself. I thought it was the coolest thing ever. So, anyway, I brought my sax and the guys of the band noticed the shape of the case and asked what it was I played. Long story short, we jammed the night away and had drinks afterwards. I kept coming back to New Orleans after that. Even thought about buying an apartment there, but by that time, I met Kate and things turned out differently."

"She was a student of yours, correct?"

"Yes, but we didn't start to date until after she graduated. And even then, it was frowned upon. First time I laid eyes on her, I couldn't believe the power that was emanating from her. I've never felt anything like it. I had met other elementals before, but never anything like her. Never someone who had all the elements inside her. Yes, I was hooked from the beginning. I'm sorry, you probably don't want to hear this at all."

Eve shook her head. "No, it's fine. Come on, Alan. We're both of a certain age. We both come with a lot of history. I knew from the start Kate means a lot to you." She fell silent when Danny came back with their orders.

"One Clam Chowder for the lady with two skewers on the side. And Shrimper's Heaven for you, sir. Do you need a refill?"

"Yes, please," Alan replied. Once Danny had left their table, he continued. "Yes, I do still care for Kate, though not in the way you think. Not anymore. I know you worry about that, I felt it several times."

She was about to protest, when Alan reached for her hand again. "It's okay. I just want you to know I don't see Kate like that anymore. As a potential lover, I mean. Do I care about her, what happens to her? In a way, even love her? Yes, I think a part of me always will. We shared so much. It's more a brotherly sort of love now, though. I hope, very much, that one day I can call her a friend again."

"Are you worried about the painting?"

"I was. Especially when it almost choked me to death the moment she disappeared into it. I hadn't realised I was still tied to her energy that much. I'll be prepared for that in the future now. And yes, of course, I'm worried. I have to believe, however, that if this was all set up by her grandmother, she means her no harm and will find a way to return her safe and sound into our world. What has me worried is Kate's reaction. She usually has a pretty good handle on her elements, but we all have our limits. This might be one of Kate's. Like I said, she hates being lied to, injustice, that sort of thing."

"So, what were you and Roy talking about for so long?"

"Leah gave him a lot of interesting information. I think he was trying to distract her as well, to keep her from worrying about Kate too much. We already know Leah saw the ball, dropping too fast." He stopped talking.

Eve turned around and saw Danny coming over, carrying their drinks.

"Thank you," they both said simultaneously, which made them laugh.

Danny gave them a big smile. "Enjoy, folks. Let me know if you need anything else!"

"She saw something else?" Eve guessed as much. Leah would have been focussing on this particular event. Their seers always saw more when they focussed. Though she got the feeling Leah outshone their own seers by a mile. Well, with exception of the Serpent, of course.

"She did. Not only did it drop too fast, it exploded at the bottom. Besides the damage that this will obviously cost, just think of all the millions of little crystals flying around at high speed. Besides that, she saw some sort of cloudy stuff coming from the ball. The next vision she had was of people choking on the ground." He almost whispered the last part.

Eve knew she must look horrified. She spoke in a soft voice, "You mean like a virus? Or some sort of poison?"

Alan shrugged. "She doesn't know. It could be either. Whatever's inside that ball, though, it can't be good. My guess is, it's already in place. It has to be. We know everything's already set up for the big event. No way someone is getting alone time with that ball from now until New Year's."

"Body count?"

"She told Roy thousands. Both from the explosion and from whatever's inside that damn thing."

"Lovely. Just lovely. For once, I would like a normal year. Well, at least this is probably coming from a normal group. One country trying to screw over another? That would explain the getting all inventive part and go for mass-murder. Ugh." She took a sip from her rum cocktail. Somehow it tasted a little bitter right now.

"A normal group?" he almost hissed. "You're calling this a normal group. What's normal about freaking mass-murder? Okay, I suppose the US has plenty of enemies. Get in line, basically, but still."

"True," she said in a contemplating voice. "Hmm, I do hope your guy delivers. If we are dealing with terrorists, chances are he will find something."

Alan stared at her. "God, you say that like it's business as usual. I'd much rather be dealing with, well, our kind of people."

Eve smiled at him. "Trust me on this, you don't. Really. Our kind are unpredictable and, depending on their abilities and strength, much harder to track down and stop. Terrorists are committed to the cause. Most of them don't care whether they live or die, which makes them dangerous, but their ammo is pretty straightforward. It makes it easier to track them down. Well, for our company, that is."

"But, besides Tristan, Charles and Roy, we don't really have all the resources of the Company, now do we? And I thought you said Tristan had been demoted?"

"Yes, though that won't matter when it comes to terrorists. Our clearance level has more to do with all the weird stuff that exists in our world and we don't want people to know about." She gave him a wink. "You know, elementals who have to stop asteroids.

That sort of thing."

Alan rolled his eyes.

"Was there anything else, anything that can give us a lead? Did she see any faces, a smell, a sound perhaps? I know she's good. Don't get me wrong, but I'm not too fond of seers. In my experience, they cause more problems than they solve."

"I can only share from my own experience. I will say this, though. Leah is one of the most down-to-earth people I've ever met. She will never share anything she's not one hundred percent sure of. She's actually one of the few people I approved of while Kate and I were dating."

"Do you know any of the others?"

"Of her current group, you mean? No, not really. I met Deborah several times back in the Netherlands, but that was after Kate and I had broken up. She hates my guts. The feeling is mutual, by the way. She gets on my nerves. I never met anyone else of her current circle. I always had a feeling I would have liked Meg, though."

"Did Meg live in the Netherlands as well?"

"Oh no, and we never met. Kate always spoke very highly of her and of course, with what she could do, I was more than a little interested. I always wondered if I could have trained her to become another master of death."

"Oh! You really think so? Is that how it begun for you as well? Seeing death, I mean?"

He nodded. "Yes. And it actually took me a really long time to figure out I could do more than that. Not after what they did to my parents."

"I'm sorry, Alan. Tristan told me about that."

"Stupid thing was, they just got in the way. A simple robbery, only they got back home too soon. Dinner and a show, only the show had been cancelled. My dad jumped in front of my mother to protect her and they beat him up pretty bad, but they hurt my mother in the most terrible way imaginable, just for good measure.

Needless to say, I returned the favour tenfold and killed them all, you know, for good measure. I had actually bought a gun. When you're an empath, it's not hard to get one. It was supposed to be a clean kill. I was so angry. I remember the fury building inside of me, wishing them dead, crushing their hearts. The first guy dropped to the floor, just like that. He was dead instantly. I remember being shocked, that I had done that. Because I immediately knew that had been my doing, my willpower. I probably would have walked away and left the other two alone, only one of them had a gun as well and he pointed it straight at me. Well, that brought back the fury and the rest is history as they say."

"Damn! You know we've never met anyone like you, right? There were always rumours, of course. I mean, if I can revive people, there had to be a flipside, right? Someone who could do exactly the opposite? I didn't realise it took you so many years to find out. And what a way to find out. It must have been the ultimate high and low all at the same time. Were you scared?"

"Of what I could do? Yes, a bit. I did not know to what extent my powers reached. I have to admit, I started to experiment after that. Small things, you know. Giving people a headache, sometimes even unconsciously. I remember a colleague of mine who always made me sick to my stomach. She had been getting on my nerves again and suddenly she was the one puking her guts out. That's when I realised I could pretty much do anything. It's interesting what you said about flipside, though. I never thought of it that way, but of course, that's exactly what your powers are. Have you ever met another reviver?"

Eve shook her head. "No. Never. And believe me, the Company searched. A lot. Being the only one makes me a liability, you see. There's a reason why I always get to do things my way. Well, most of the time, anyway. It's very simple, though. They do not have a backup. There's only one me. I think that is…" She stopped talking when she felt her new burner phone vibrate. She took it out and saw she had a text message. It just contained a few words. She exhaled and showed it to Alan.

She's back! Keep you posted. R

Tristan

Catherine was struggling to get up from the floor. She was hurting, and she could hardly breathe. Tristan could feel it and the panic building inside of him. Tristan barked instructions. "Give her some space, people. Back off. Sue, get your ass in here now!"

Sue came flying through the door. She started hovering her hands over Catherine's body immediately. Her breathing was slowing down. Tristan had his powers on full force, so he could pick up on even the smallest change. She started to breathe more easily. Her eyes searched the room frantically until they found his own. She kept staring at him like he was her anchor. Yes, definitely bad, whether or not it was just physical, he could not tell. He waited for Sue to say something.

"Nothing's broken. Her breathing was off. One of her lungs collapsed, and she was having some form of motion sickness. Not unlike people I've encountered who had to deal with a certain amount of G-force. I've fixed the lung. Kate, honey, can you hear me? Are you in pain? Just blink once for yes, twice for no."

They both saw Catherine blink twice, slowly, but deliberately. Tristan relaxed just a bit more. She was okay, physically, at least. Her eyes never left his.

"Okay, is it safe to move her, Sue?"

Sue nodded. "Yes, I think so. Be careful, though. We don't want to start the nausea again."

"Right." Tristan looked at the bed, but there was just no way he was leaving her in the same room as that blasted painting. She'd probably feel better in her own room anyway. "Sweetie, can you put your arm around me? I'm going to carry you to our own room, okay?"

Catherine blinked once. Tristan lifted her carefully from the floor. She weighed almost next to nothing. He carefully walked to her room, passing Sue and Leah, Deborah and Catherine's mother by the door. Thankfully Leah had managed to keep everyone else from coming up to check upon Catherine. Tristan gently laid Catherine down on the bed and put two pillows behind her so she could sit up a little straighter.

"My throat hurts," she croaked.

"On it!" Deborah answered, already rushing down the stairs. Catherine's mother hovered in the door opening.

"Are you okay, honey?" Her eyes were awfully shiny. Catherine nodded and looked down again. Tristan picked up on her anxiety. "Mrs. van Dyk, could you ask Deborah if she could also bring some honey up here? It might soothe her throat."

"Of course. I'll be right back, sweetheart."

Tristan looked at Leah. "Any chance you can explain to the rest she's at least doing okay? They must be frantic downstairs."

Leah nodded. "I was just thinking the same thing. You take care of our girl, okay?"

Tristan looked her straight in the eye. "Count on it."

As soon as Leah had left the room as well, he turned to Catherine. "Are you okay? Can you talk? Do you need me to get everyone out of here? Just nod and I will."

A tear rolled down her cheek, and he gently wiped it away.

"How am I ever going to hide this from them, Tristan?" she whispered so softly that he could hardly hear her.

"Catherine? Catherine, look at me." He waited until she looked into his eyes. "You don't have to do anything you don't want to do, you hear me? But you have to tell me how you want to proceed here and we don't have a lot of time. Now, I don't know what was said, and that's between you and your grandmother." She winced as he mentioned her name. "If you want to keep this a secret for now, I will help you. If you want to tell them, I'll back you up."

Catherine looked desperate. "I cannot tell her. It will kill her. I wouldn't even know how to start." Her breathing became ragged again. He immediately understood she meant her mother.

"Breathe, sweetie, breathe. We're going with keeping it a secret for now, okay? You can always decide upon a different course later on." She nodded her consent. "Good girl. Now look into my eyes. I'm going to take all the pain and the anxiety away, just for now. It will feel strange, like something is muted because I don't want to deprive you of your emotions entirely, but it will give you focus. Do you understand?" She nodded again. He gently probed her mind and found what he was looking for. He visualised a big old-fashioned trunk for her, and she picked up on his intentions straight away. Opening the box, she put the emotions in herself and he helped her to close the lid on the trunk. Once they were done, he pulled out of her mind and looked into her eyes. She gave him a soft, calm smile.

Catherine's mother returned with the tea. "Here you go, sweetheart. fresh camomile tea with honey. Deborah cooled it down, so you should be able to drink it straightaway. Just, small sips."

Tristan took the mug from her and gave it to Catherine. She took a small sip and then another one.

"That feels good," she said, her voice still a bit hoarse, but stronger.

"Oh, my darling, we've been so worried!" her mother exclaimed. "How did you find your way back?"

"Perhaps we should give Catherine some rest before we start on the third degree?" Tristan's voice was gentle, but there was an underlying warning. He wouldn't let anyone upset her, not even her mother.

"No, Tristan, it's okay. Really. I'm not sure myself, Mom. I just felt a sort of big push and then suddenly everything sped up and I was lying on the floor. I won't be trying that again, though. It hurt like hell. Remind me to thank Sue for patching me up, yet again."

"Don't talk too much. You'll wear yourself out," Tristan said to her.

"Do you remember anything? Anything at all?" Deborah had come back in. "Lee's keeping everybody calm downstairs. I guess we're not cutting that cake then, right?"

"How long was I gone?" Catherine asked.

"Couple of hours," Deborah answered before Tristan had the chance. "Good thing you made it home by midnight. We were considering the nightmare version of Cinderella. I don't think the pumpkin look would have worked for you. Doesn't go with your complexion."

Catherine gave her a smile. "As for your question, I'm not sure, Deb. It's all very blurry, like a Monet, you know?"

Deborah nodded. "Yeah, pretty from afar, but a big mess up close. I can tell you one thing, though. That thing is going. You're not keeping it here any longer. Are we clear?"

Catherine nodded. "Yes, ma'am. Actually, I was thinking Tristan could take it for examination to the Company? See if they can find anything useful? Maybe they can provide us with some answers?"

Clever girl, he thought. "That is an excellent idea. And I couldn't agree more with Deborah. The painting has to go. Roy and Charles will deal with it."

Deborah hesitated. "Lee thinks it might be better to cancel our New York trip, Kate."

Catherine sat up straighter. "No." Her voice was suddenly a lot stronger. "Not gonna happen, Deb, we're going. Honestly, I'm feeling better by the minute."

Deborah still looked doubtful. "You're absolutely sure? Seven to eight hours in a plane is not the greatest place to be when you're recovering."

"For goodness sake, people. I'm not sick or anything. Besides, eight hours, that's four movies. I'm sure I'll live. Even with the bad coffee. Not to mention we're flying business class. I've had way worse. We both have."

Deborah nodded and sighed.

"Okay. For the record, I asked. I told Lee you wouldn't listen."

"She gets that stubbornness from her grandmother. It must have skipped a generation," her mother said in a huff.

"Not bloody likely," Catherine mumbled under her breath. Tristan bit back a smile.

"Did you say something, honey?" her mother asked.

"Nothing, Mom. Do you think I should go down and explain I'm okay?"

"Nonsense. I think Leah has probably done a great job explaining the situation. And besides, since you're such a stubborn girl, most of them will see you tomorrow anyway. I'll get everybody out of your hair. You make sure you get a good night's sleep." The last part she said with a glare towards Tristan.

"I'll make sure she's rested and fully restored before she gets on that plane, ma'am. You have my word." No one could doubt the sincerity in Tristan's voice and Catherine's mother looked satisfied.

"Good, good. Now you take care, darling." Her mom gave her a gentle hug.

"I'm sorry I hardly had any time to catch up with Simon and Uncle Ben. Will you give them my love, Mom?"

"Of course, my dear. And don't worry about that. We'll see you in the new year. Will you Skype us?"

"Sure, Mom. If the connection holds, that is. Americans can get a bit crazy when it comes to the new year. Besides, you'll be celebrating much earlier."

"Oh right, time difference. I'll never get used to that. Well, let me know when you're safely on the ground in New York and enjoy your stay. I do hope you'll feel better. You still look a bit peaky."

Catherine sighed. "I'm fine, Mom."

"Yes, yes, I'll get out of your hair. Goodnight, darling."

"Night, mom. Love you." Catherine blew her a kiss. Her mother gave her a smile and nodded to Tristan.

"I'll walk you to the door, Elizabeth," Deborah said to her. "Kate, call us when you're awake, okay? I'll tell Leah. I assume I'll see you in the morning as well, Tristan?" She looked at him.

He nodded. "Yes, thank you, Deborah. I'll take care of her."

"I know," she said with a smile.

Deborah and Mrs. van Dyk left the room, and he could hear them walking down the stairs and a soft buzzing from different types of voices. He could not make our what was being said. He heard footsteps on the stairs again. A moment later Roy's head peeked around the corner.

"Getting that painting out of here, boss. Hey, Kate, you look terrible."

Catherine rolled her eyes. "Yes, nice to see you too, Roy. You can burn that thing, for all I care."

He laughed. "I think the rightful owner wouldn't like that very much, Kate, but we'll make sure it won't be bothering you anytime soon. Feel better!"

Tristan and Catherine remained silent for a while. They could hear Roy and Charles down the hallway and more people downstairs. Slowly the noise retreated and finally they heard the door close for the last time.

"Alone at last." He smiled at her. "Still feeling okay? Do you want to open the trunk?"

Catherine shook her head. "No, I don't think that's wise. I kind of like being able to think straight."

He nodded his agreement. "I can't imagine what you've must have gone through. It must have been such a shock." His voice sounded sad, even to him.

"Honestly, I didn't believe any of it, at first. I just thought I was in some weird sort of dream world. Or like astral travel even. But she knew things she couldn't have picked out of my memories." She looked up at him. "Did you know she wants me to take over?"

He stared at her. "Take over the Company? No, I did not know that. I thought she wanted to recruit you. Which I was against, by the way. Catherine, I swear to you right here and now, I never, until very recently, knew my company was being led by your grandmother."

"I know," she whispered. "And I know why you couldn't tell me when you did find out. Hell, I'm not even sure I would have believed you. I might have thought you'd lost your marbles and sent for Sue." She sat up straight un the bed and pulled her legs in. "Can I ask you why you're against my recruitment? Do you think I would not be suitable?"

He looked at her in amazement. "That's the first thing you want to know? Why I think you're not Company material? Well, for one thing because you hate keeping secrets. My whole life is one big secret, Catherine."

"Oh, right. I thought it might have been something else." She looked a bit embarrassed. He picked up on it straightaway.

"You really thought I would find you unqualified? Well, in a sense that is true, I suppose. Blowing our cover to kingdom come in the first week would be a bit of a setback." He gave her a wink and took her hand into his. "But no, I never thought you wouldn't be able to hold your own. I just don't think my life would make you happy."

"Maybe I'd be happy anywhere, as long as you're there."

He frowned. "That's a dangerous way to look at life, Catherine."

"Why?" she asked, a stubborn look in her eyes.

"Because," he sighed, "those kinds of sentiments are exactly what makes you an easy target. Or the people you love."

"Oh," was all the reply he got. She clearly had her own ideas about that, and he could feel them forming a more solid picture as they spoke. He sighed. Stubborn indeed.

"Nana asked me to visit her tomorrow morning, before we leave for New York. She also said Lee and Deb would be coming with me because they would not let me visit the Company alone."

He looked at her. "Did she now? Well, she is the greatest seer in the world, so I guess it's safe to say she's right about that. It sure sounds like Deborah and Leah. I wouldn't let you go alone, either. What else did she say?"

"She said she made a mistake with Alan. Or no, not exactly, with Alan and me. He was supposed to train me becoming a master of death. She never saw me attacking him, you know. It wasn't supposed to happen that way. That's why she changed plans and brought you into the equation and why she put a lot of effort in reviving Alan. Apparently, when I was a little girl, she already saw the asteroid. Every outcome she could possibly see, ended in my death, no matter what she changed. Then she started to look for other people like herself and decided to fake her own death. It created another vision. Another future. One that still ended up with my being dead, but with someone there who would be able to revive me."

"Eve. She found Eve." He pulled his hands through his hair. "Eve was basically brought in at a very young age. Her background isn't a happy one. The Company pretty much became her family."

"Sounds very X-Men. That's sad, though, about her childhood, I mean."

He nodded. "Hmm, yes. It is. She's over it, though, so don't feel too bad. Well, I have to say, I'm quite impressed with the lengths she went through to keep you safe. Still, my world isn't a happy world, Catherine. And I think it's safe to say none of our hands are clean. That would most certainly include your grandmother."

Her chin came up.

"I know that. In fact, I'm pretty sure she had someone killed over that blasted painting. She implied something that made my skin crawl. Something you would be able to confirm. Dammit, I can't remember clearly what she said about that."

Goddammit! I knew it. I fucking knew it. It had been Alan on that bike. Okay, keep it together. Not worth the trouble. Let it go.

He frowned. "We were never involved with the actual painting. My team tried to get as much intel on it as we possibly could, but one of my informers ended up dead before we received the information we were looking for. They found his body in the Thames. I'm not sure that's related, though. We always thought another party was working against us. It's not uncommon in our line of work."

She had a look of concentration on her face. He could feel her mind jumping from one emotion to another. "What are you thinking?"

"I don't think it was another party. I think this was your own Company. You said you were looking for intel on the painting? Anything that could explain why it was showing up in my dreams? I think I know what your informer found out. She ordered Alan to retrieve to information from you before you could read it, you know. She didn't say he killed for it, though."

He stared at her, having already come to that conclusion it had been Alan on that bike. "Do tell, the suspense is killing me, you know."

"The painting is a twin. There are two of them. That's how they create a portal. The other one is in her office. At least, that's what she said. She must have known if you'd find out, you would put two and two together, consider the painting too dangerous and have it taken from my apartment. And, obviously, she needed the painting to create a 'safe space' to meet me. Ugh, I never imagined my grandmother would be capable of murder. Or, give the order at the very least. I'm so sorry for the life of your informer, Tristan. Did he have a family?"

"No." He looked away, pulling himself together. After a moment's hesitation, he continued, "He wasn't exactly squeaky clean, but he was not a bad guy. However, to be honest, I don't think it was Alan who killed him. We checked, Alan could have gotten rid of him in a much easier way, even without his powers of death. He's an empath, after all. No, she sent someone else. For the greater good, right?"

She looked horrified.

"There. That's the look I've been waiting for. This is what I mean, Catherine. Is this really the life you want to be living?" Now she had that look again. Determination.

"I could change things, do things my way."

"Ha! Now there's a fight I would love to see. Your grandmother built the Company from the ground up, Catherine. She won't just hand you the keys and have fun with it. Too much depends on it. Too many lives depend on it."

"I know that," she said irritably. "I'm not some ignorant child, you know. I do know a thing or two about bad guys." He raised a brow.

"Do you now?" he said to her in a teasing voice.

"Yes, I do. Or have you forgotten my time with Alan and his obsession with tracking down evil people?" That wiped the smile right off his face. No, he most certainly had not forgotten that little piece of information.

"I'm sorry. I did not mean to belittle you. The point I was trying to make—quite inadequately I might add—was that you chose to walk away from that situation as well. You're a force for good, Catherine. You're all about justice and honesty. Hell, that's what I love about you. My world, it's all about deception and secrets."

"Okay, point taken. Still, how are we going to handle this tomorrow morning?"

"Well, I could mention we have information on the ball drop. Which we will probably have by the morning. Alan and Eve are working on that. Shh. I'll tell you later," he said when she was about to interrupt him. "Charles can pick us up. Official Company car and all that. Probably best to have your suitcase packed and ready to go. We don't know how long you'll be there, and you don't want the stress of arriving at the airport too late."

Catherine snorted.

"No, that would freak Leah out, for sure. She's not the most relaxed travelling companion known to mankind. But I have to ask, Alan and Eve are in New York already? Together?"

Tristan nodded. "Hmm, yes. Perhaps another thing your grandmother hadn't quite accounted for. Or perhaps she did, I don't know. I've already told you Eve revived you, and I decided to give them a head start. Well, they've been together ever since, and it seems they've taken quite a shine to one another."

Catherine's mouth fell open. "Come again? No way! Oh, this is getting way too weird. So, what exactly? My ex is hooking up with your ex?"

He shrugged. "Seems like it. Does it bother you?"

She frowned. "Bother me? No, I don't think so. Why would it bother me?" She rubbed her chin. "That's a pretty powerful combination. A reviver and a master of death, who also happens to be an empath. Impossible to beat, I would say. Remind me to stay on their good side."

He smiled. "I don't think that will be a problem. Alan still thinks very highly of you and Eve, well, you're starting to grow on her. That has more to do with how she feels about me than anything with your own character."

"Oh. I get that. She's protective of you. I would feel the same. Well, I'm determined to like her, I'm in her debt, after all. I owe her my life."

He shook his head. "That's what she does. You don't owe her anything. She won't see it like that."

"Well, I do." There was that stubborn look again. Suddenly, it was gone. "I would actually like it very much if I could get a chance to speak to Alan again. I need to apologize to him. I've been feeling awful, ever since I found out he never meant to hurt me. He needs to hear that. From me," she added.

"I'm sure you'll get that chance pretty soon. They moved into one of the hotels near Leah's home. Roy is arranging a flight for us as we speak."

"You're coming to New York?" she said, sounding happy.

"You really think I would let you go alone with this whole ball drop mess? Not a chance. Besides, I have a feeling that's exactly what your grandmother wants, us working together on this."

"And by us, you mean not just you and me, but Alan and Eve as well. She knows you let them go."

He nodded. "Of course, she knows. Part of her plan, no doubt. But, Catherine, this isn't something supernatural we're up against. This is most likely plain terrorism. People, committed to a cause, for whatever reason. Before you say anything, I know you're a very capable woman, but you're not bulletproof and you have no training dealing with these sorts of people. If, and that is a big if, we're going to be working on this together, I will need your word you won't do anything without my knowledge. I will promise you the same in return."

"Sounds reasonable. You're not entirely right, though. Bullets fly through the air. I control air. I'm not saying I could stop hundreds of AK47's at the same time, but I'm pretty sure I could stop or redirect a flying bullet."

Tristan let that sink in. "That could actually come in pretty handy. Still, a theory I would rather not test, if you don't mind."

"What, you don't have blanks at the Company?"

"Catherine, let it go for now, okay? Do you think you can behave for five minutes and not endanger yourself? I need to fill in Roy and Charles, and I'm sure Roy has news for me as well. After that, I think we both could use some shut-eye. Tomorrow's going to be a long day."

"Just some shut-eye?" she asked, an innocent look on her face.

Damn that woman.

"You'll be the death of me, I swear," he said before pulling out his phone and calling Roy.

Alan

"I still can't get over the fact she didn't go completely bonkers," Alan said to Eve for the third time. She rolled her eyes.

"Did you really expect that she would blow up the painting, or the Company, for that matter?"

"Honestly? Yes, pretty much! I thought she would be mad as a snake. Finding out she has been manipulated most of her life? I mean, damn, that would even get under my skin."

"Yes, well, it might be wise not to mention it to her in that particular way. If she's looking at this differently, I say that's a good thing, right?"

"Can't believe she actually wants to see me," he mumbled. Eve had told him what Roy had told her. They were still flying out to New York tomorrow, after having breakfast with dear old Grams. He wondered how that would go down. Kate's lung had collapsed from the impact crashing back into this world. He wasn't very pleased about that. Stupid wench could not have foreseen that? He supposed she had, with Sue being there to heal her, but still. Careless. She could have been wrong.

"Yes, I know you're happy about that. I am too. You two deserve a chance to patch things up." She smiled at him. He didn't feel any envy or jealousy. Amazing woman.

"You're really okay with that? You know I do not see her in that way anymore, right?"

"I know that, darling. I wish you would give me the same credit when it comes to Tristan, though. That would be a nice gesture on your part."

He made a tutting noise. "Yes, well, I will try. It's a man thing. I'm sure Tristan is not so charitable towards me, either."

"A man thing?" She raised a perfectly manicured eyebrow at him, and he could feel the irritation building up inside her. Time from some backpedaling.

"I just mean women tend to be more reasonable about matters of the heart. We men are just plain stupid. Too much testosterone." He looked at her sheepishly.

"Nice save," she said.

"Hmm, I thought so too," he replied. "If I'd known what that painting could do, I'm not sure I would have delivered it to her apartment."

"And as with all these things, the interesting question is, would we still be here if you hadn't? Every decision changes the future, after all. Some have a greater impact, some none at all, but it makes you wonder, though."

"Indeed, but if I think too long about such things, my head starts to hurt. Besides, I like the whole free will theory."

"Oh, I think we have free will. I also think life has a funny way of getting what it wants as well. Don't me ask me how that works. I'm not much of a philosopher."

"Anyway, what I've been meaning to ask, can we move around more freely now? With Kate's grandmother wanting us to work together and all, that's pretty hard when there's a price on your head, so to speak."

"Oh, they still want me back, that hasn't changed. Besides, she wants us to work together. That doesn't mean she has revoked the chase on us. However, Roy did confirm that for as long as we are working together here in New York, she would call off the teams chasing after us."

"Well, that's something, at least. I asked because we can hardly set up shop here in this room. I was thinking about Leah's place."

"And scare the living shit out of Ryan? Good idea. Let's just show up on his doorstep." She rolled her eyes. "Ryan, her partner? Ring any bells?"

"No, sorry. When Leah and I knew each other, she was a single woman. I had no idea she was married."

"Well, they're not actually married, but they've been living together for quite some time now. Ryan Walker, he's an executive officer at Juilliard. You know, the performing arts conservatory in New York?"

"Yes, I do know ballet, thank you very much. Everybody's heard of Juilliard."

"Not that many men I know of, love, and for the record, it's much more than just ballet, but you never stop surprising me."

It was his turn to roll his eyes. "Good for Leah. Sounds like her kind of man. I do see your point, though. He does know what she can do, right?"

"Yes, no secrets there, though I got the impression from Tristan it's not something they talk about very often. He's away a lot and obviously, so is she."

Does he…," he started to ask, but Eve shook her head, probably hearing the question in his mind.

"No, Ryan is as common as they come. You know what I mean. Actually, he used to be quite a talented dancer before he became an executive officer, and I'm sure he has many other hidden talents. The supernatural kind are not among them, though. Of that, we're sure. The Company is always very thorough."

"As if I needed reminding of that," he said, but his voice was gentle. "Okay, so ringing the bell unannounced might not be the greatest idea."

"I don't even know if he's at home. He might be away on business. We have an office here, you know. In New York. Of course, I will have to check with Roy if he's absolutely sure they won't try to lock us up and throw away the key the minute we set foot in the building, but I don't see why we couldn't 'set up shop,' as you put it, over there?"

"Is it anywhere close by?" Alan asked.

"No, unfortunately not. We're not even anywhere near Manhattan. The office is located in Brooklyn, near Coney Island."

"Bugger, that's a long way from here. I thought the Company had money to burn. Why not Manhattan?"

"Because we also like to be practical, and Manhattan is absolute murder trying to make a quick getaway when necessary."

"Ah, I see. Can you show me on a map?"

"Sure," she said, grabbing the New York map provided by the hotel. "Okay, so, we're here," she pointed at the hotel, "and the Company is located over here. You see Emmons Avenue, near Sheepshead Bay? There. We have the entire top floor of that building. So no, money is not exactly an issue."

"Must be nice." He rubbed his eyes. "Remind me we keep the sound of my phone on. I'm not sure how much longer I can stay awake. Those cocktails might not have been the brightest idea."

"We could go and get a coffee somewhere. We could take the B train towards Brighton Beach, but it will take us over an hour."

"Good grief! You weren't kidding when you said on the other side of town. Isn't there a faster way?"

Eve grinned. "Sure, if you're up for it?"

He wasn't sure he liked the look in her eye.

* * *

Alan was in his element. He was racing through the city, following Eve, watching her weave through traffic. This was so much better than sitting on a stupid train. The motorcycle beneath him purred like a kitten. He loved Ducati. He was absolutely clueless as to how she got these so fast. She'd also texted Roy to check if they could try their luck at Emmons Avenue, and Roy had said they should be able to get in with Eve's access codes. A grin spread across his face when he remembered the time Tristan had chased him across London. That had been sweet. Okay, the Millennium Bridge might not have been his brightest idea, but he had been counting on Tristan to slow down because of all the people on the bridge. Apparently, Tristan had a competitive streak in him as well because he'd been hot on his tail. He had told Eve about that chase, and she'd just looked at him and smiled.

It was relatively quiet on the road. Well, quiet for New York he supposed. If they didn't want the NYPD on their heels, they couldn't run the risk of speeding. The wind felt good, though. Back at the hotel, he'd really been worried about staying awake long enough to give Marcello a call. Now, the sleep deprivation was under control again. He noticed Eve speeding up in front of him not to run a red light, and he followed suit. They made it to Coney Island in just over half an hour. Even with the lights, Sheepshead Bay looked pitch-black, like a shining dark mirror. Eve drove into an underground parking garage. Alan followed and parked next to her.

"That was precisely what I needed!" he said, taking off his helmet. "But tell me, how did you get these bikes at this hour? Did you steal them? Like the police uniforms?"

Eve rolled her eyes and laughed out loud at him. "You're kidding, right? The Company does come with some perks, you know. No, hon, they're not stolen. They belong to the Company. Now let's see if my security code works."

"You're absolutely sure Roy said this would work, right?"

"That's what he said, yes. If the Serpent has an agenda of her own, well, we're about to find out." Eve walked up to the door in the garage. It opened when she pressed her thumb on the panel. "So far, so good, I suppose." The door led to a stone staircase and they started to walk up the stairs. Soon they reached ground level with a larger door, probably leading to the building's lobby.

"Do you want to keep climbing to the top floor or do you want to press our luck and see what's behind door number two?" Alan asked.

"I'm feeling adventurous, aren't you?" she winked and pulled the door open. They were in a spacious room with a lobby in the middle, as they had expected. No one was at the desk, though.

The space was abandoned. "Maybe there's only someone at the desk during the day? Come on, let's go to the lifts."

"Elevators," he automatically replied.

What?" she asked.

"They call them elevators here," Alan said. She rolled her eyes at him and shrugged.

"Whatever, let's go." She pressed the top floor.

"*You've reached Serpent Enterprises*," a female voice said through the speakers.

"Guess we're in the right place then," Eve said and stepped out of the lift. There was a glass wall across the entire floor with a big door in the middle. Another panel was right next to it. "Okay, here we go."

This panel also contained digits besides the scan for thumb and fingerprints. Alan saw Eve push her entire hand down on the panel. The panel flashed green and was now asking for her digit code. She pressed several numbers and hit the okay button. The panel flashed green again, and they heard the door click.

"And we're in. Come on, let's go check it out," Eve said, and he had to smile. He could hear the excitement in her voice. This was so her thing. Skulking around in places she wasn't supposed to be. Even though this still was her job, technically. It wasn't like they had fired her. Hell, if anything, they wanted her back. Still, he could sense she got a thrill out of being at the Company, even though it was not headquarters, so to speak. She walked through the hallway, flipping on lights as she went along, peeking inside an office or two. They all had panels attached next to the door, but most of the doors were open. Finally, she seemed to have found what she was looking for.

"Perfect," Eve said. It looked like an empty office. Two big desks, two monitor screens, two keyboards, but this was not a clean desk policy. There was absolutely nothing else in the room. He was just about to ask whether or not the office was in use when

Eve continued, "It's obviously not in use, so we can take this one. I'll clear it with Tristan as soon as they get here."

She started unzipping her backpack. He hadn't even noticed she'd brought it along. She plugged her laptop in alongside the monitor and hit the keyboard. The monitors sprang to life, showing a logo. It looked like caduceus, the staff of Hermes, the god of travellers and messages from ancient Greece. Only instead of two wings, it contained the symbol of the triquetra at the top. It kept rotating on the screen. He'd seen it many times on ancient rune stones in Northern Europe and knew it held meaning to both the pagan and the Christian world.

"Nice logo," he commented.

Eve looked around. "The Company logo? Yes, I suppose. Never given it that much thought. It's why we always refer to the big boss as the Serpent."

"It reminds me of the staff of Hermes, only the top is different. Did you know it is said the wand of Hermes could wake the sleeping and send the awake to sleep? And if applied to someone who was dying, their death would be gentle. However, if the wand was used on the dead, they returned to life."

Eve stopped tapping the keyboard. "Really? So, the wand could revive?"

"That's what legend tells us, yes."

"You're really interested in this sort of thing, aren't you?" she asked him, returning her attention to the screen. He smiled, though she couldn't see it.

"Symbolism, you mean? Yes, symbolism can tell you a great deal about the people who use it. And I'm always interested in the way the human mind works. Where people draw power from, or give power to. In my experience, a sacred place is exactly that because people give it their own power, they feed it and, therefore, it becomes sacred."

"Interesting theory. Would you be a dear and see if you can find a printer anywhere nearby?"

"Sure," he said, moving out of the room and checking the nearest office. There was a printer right in the corner. He was just about to turn around when he heard a noise down the hallway. Alan froze. It was too late to notify Eve. He kept on walking and relaxed. It was just a security guard, probably doing his rounds. Alan looked at his nametag. It read Steve Johnson. He reached out with his mind and planted the thought of familiarity. *You know me, Steve. Remember? Paul from upstairs. You like me.*

Alan walked to the door and opened it. "Hiya, Steve. How are you? We're working late tonight."

The security guard looked a bit dazed but replied nonetheless. "No problem, Paul. Just doing my rounds and saw the lights were on. It's usually dark here after working hours. Are they putting you through the ringer?"

"Yes, good thing they pay us overtime," Alan said with a wink.

The guard smiled back at him. "Be thankful it doesn't happen very often. Well, don't let me keep you, Paul. You have a good night now."

"Thanks, Steve. Same to you."

Steve tapped his hat in salute. "Don't forget to lock up behind you."

"Will do!" Alan said, tapping his hand to his head before closing the door again. He walked back slowly, taking him time. Eve was just around the corner, holding a gun in her hand.

"Where the hell did you get that? Put that away. It was just a security guard doing his rounds. Nothing I can't handle, Eve." He felt her relax, and she lowered the gun.

"I got it from the safe. I heard you talking to someone, and I thought it would be better to be safe than sorry."

"Christ, Eve! Overreact much?"

"Yes, well, that's easy for you to say. I may be able to read minds, but I can't control them, okay. I've learned to defend myself a long time ago."

"Okay, okay, take it easy. Look, I would never let them get near you, I know this is new for the both of us. But if we're going to stay together, we have to start trusting each other with our lives as well."

"You're right. Of course, you're right. My defence mechanism just kicked in, that's all. Still, it couldn't hurt to keep this with us."

Alan frowned. "In my experience, guns usually end up being used against you."

"Then it's probably time you learned how to use one." Eve's voice held no accusation, but he could feel she was being serious.

"I do know how to handle a gun. I did my service in the Dutch army. However, with my kind of power, it seems a bit, I don't know, overkill? No pun intended." He gave her a smile.

"Point taken. However, sometimes a situation might actually be better explained with a gun present than your specific talents. I'm just saying."

"Hmm, I never looked at it that way. In your words, point taken. So, what is it were doing here? Are you looking for something specific?"

Eve nodded. "Come take a look. I'm plugged in to the mainframe of the Company now. So, this monitor is scanning for anything that stands out on terrorist activity in New York or the United States in general. That's tapped into MI5. The monitor on the right is scanning for anything our own seers have predicted so far. Don't put too much faith in that one."

Alan knew Eve wasn't a big fan of the Company's seers. His best guess was they had screwed up too many times to be a reliable source for her. She didn't like to talk about it. It made her irritable.

She continued, "This one, though, on my own laptop, hopefully will come up with something useful. You see, it's scanning for patterns."

"Like some sort of profiling?" he asked.

"Yes, sort of. It's state of the art artificial intelligence. It's able to connect people to events, location, motive. It cost the Company a fortune. One of Tristan's team members helped design it. She's very good in connecting the dots. A modern Sherlock Holmes, if you will. And the good thing about this technical version is, it will never get tired. However, I do hope he will bring her along. We could use someone with her talents."

"There's a printer in the next room, by the way. Do we need it in here?"

"Not right now, but I'd like to use this wall behind us and print out any suspects or theories we come up with. It's easier to map everything out.

"Would you like me to try Marcello? We might be lucky. Maybe he has already found something."

"Would you? Do you think you have another hour in you? I saw a coffee machine where we entered. I would like to have something prepared at least by the time they get here."

"How are we going to leave everything safe and locked up? I assume there will be people here when morning comes."

She pointed to the door. "Every door has an access panel next to it. When an office is not in us, it will be open. Company policy. I can set it to my personal code when we leave. Not even Tristan will be able to get inside."

"Hmm, I like the sound of that. Okay, coffee it is!" And he walked into the hallway.

Catherine

Everything was packed. This was the third time she checked her suitcase, carry-on luggage and handbag, and Catherine was started to feel nervous again. "Tristan!"

"Coming!" she heard him call from downstairs. He came flying up the stairs, taking two steps at a time. "Again? I calmed you down an hour ago. Not that it matters," he quickly added, probably picking up on the murderous glare she was giving him.

After just two seconds, she felt the calm blanket wrap around her and she sighed. So much better than her elements. She could work with water, which was tied to human emotions, but not like Tristan could.

"Better?" he asked. "You know, there's nothing to be worried about. I thought you were actually excited to finally see in the lion's den, so to speak?"

She sighed. "I am. But I hate keeping secrets from my friends. I'm quite sure I can never look my mother straight in the eye again. Oh, and we're about to go to New York, not to relax and celebrate the new year, but to track down a terrorist group and dismantle a million-dollar crystal ball. Also, I'll be seeing Alan within twenty-four hours after more almost a decade. Forgive me if I'm a bit on edge." She heard her voice dripping with sarcasm. That was hardly fair to Tristan. "I'm sorry. I'm not in a good mood."

"No need for apologies. I'll say it one more time, and then I promise to shut up about it. This is your choice, Catherine. It has to be your choice. I don't care which path you choose, but it does have to be your choice. No regrets. And certainly not out of fear. No matter what you choose, I *will* make sure you can lead a safe and normal life. Well, normal for you, anyway."

She smiled at him. "Whatever did I do to deserve you?" She walked over and kissed him on the lips. He responded instantly and prolonged the kiss.

"That's my line," he said, kissing the side of her neck. She was tempted to drag him back inside her bedroom and just hide there for the rest of the year, but she knew she would have to get into action soon. She sighed and slowly pulled back. He let her go.

"Charles will be here soon with Deborah and Leah. Now I doubt your grandmother will reveal herself to someone other than yourself. The Company most likely will find a way to get you alone. It's up to you if you're okay with that."

"Who will it be?" she asked. "Better to be prepared, after all."

"I'm guessing my boss, Trevor. You'll like him. He's an okay guy. Your grandmother's blocker, or stand in, I should say, not so much will also be there. At least, we didn't hit it off. That might have been me, though. I first met him after you saved the world and my guess is your grandmother gave him orders to find out how I really feel about you. Let's just say he was quite provocative. I wasn't very nice to him. His name is William. Tall, big guy, dark eyes, dark hair. I don't know if he's able to block your powers, but he could sure block mine. Be careful around him. I'm sure he won't do anything to hurt you, but his loyalties lie with your grandmother. He will protect her, probably at all costs."

"You make it sound like I'm charging in there. She said she just wanted to talk. About us, the whole New York thing, and most likely, my future. I'm sure me and William will get along fine. Don't worry about things you don't have to worry about. Worry about Lee and Deb, I still have no clue what I'm going to tell them."

"Well, decide quickly because I'm pretty sure Charles is here." On cue, Catherine's doorbell rang.

"I'll get your suitcases," Tristan said. Catherine looked around and checked the contents of her handbag one more time. Tickets, passport, keys, phone, wallet, courage. Yes, she had everything she needed.

"Okay, showtime!"

* * *

"Good grief, this place is worse than Heathrow airport," Deborah whispered to Leah, who was still waiting to get her purse back. Leah gave her friend a stare. Catherine bit back a giggle. Leah had always been a strict law-abiding citizen. Deb and herself, well, not so much. Any kind of authority still made Leah jumpy. Eventually though, they all passed the test and were allowed inside. Even Charles had made a few tutting noises, trying to speed up the process, she guessed.

It was much lighter than she had imagined and actually quite green. There were several big treelike plants in the lobby. A part of her was a bit disappointed there was no actual bat cave in sight. She had teased Tristan about having one and a part of her had actually hoped he did have a bat cave. Or at least the Company would have one. Apparently not, though. After what seemed like an endless tour of hallways, corners and lifts, they had reached Tristan office and they all stepped inside. Roy and two other people were already there.

"Kate! Is the bat cave to your liking?" Roy came over and gave her a hug. "Leah, nice to see you again. Hello, Deb." He gave both of her friends a hug as well.

Deb? Since when did that happen? She raised an eyebrow at her friend, who gave her a meaningful look, telling her to let it go.

Roy introduced them to the other two people in the room. "This is Peter, my second in command, and this here is Gilly. She's gifted, like you ladies. Gilly can see patterns. I'd introduce you, but they both know exactly who you are." He ended with a grin.

"Right, of course. It's nice to meet you both," Catherine said, giving them both a hand to shake.

"Likewise," Gilly replied softly. "It's an honour to meet a true elemental, Catherine. May I call you Catherine?"

"Oh, please, call me Kate and none of that honour crap. We're feeling pretty honoured ourselves just being allowed inside this place. Also, we never got a chance to say thank you for your assistance with the asteroid. So, thank you." She felt a wave of warmth coming from Tristan. He'd liked that.

"It was our pleasure, uhm Kate," she said, still a bit hesitant.

"Charles, how much time do we have?" Tristan asked.

"We're good on time, sir. The ladies are all flying business class with priority check-in, so we have at least two hours. Let's make the most of it now that we're here."

Tristan looked at Catherine, but the question was meant for Deborah and Leah as well. "Well, ladies, is there anything in particular you would like to see?"

"Is this a free-for-all-buffet?" Leah asked.

Roy laughed. "Why don't we find out? What do you want to see, Leah?"

Leah looked at Catherine. "If you two don't mind, I would actually be very interested to meet your seers. Would that be an option?"

"I don't see why not," Roy started to say when there was a knock on the door. Charles, who was nearest to the door, opened it.

"Good morning, people," a middle-aged man said. He scanned the room and looked Catherine in the eye. "Ah, Ms. van Dyk. A pleasure to finally meet you in the flesh. Tristan, Roy and Charles speak very highly of you."

Okay, so this must be Tristan's boss, Trevor.

"Trevor Johnsson," he said, holding out his hand. Catherine shook it. "Could I have a minute of your time, Ms. van Dyk? I would like to discuss the possibilities of getting you limited clearance for the time being." He caught her by surprise, which was reflected in Tristan's eyes as well.

"Oh! Uhm, sure." She felt Leah's hesitation, and Deborah

was already checking Trevor Johnsson for ulterior motives. She would have to say something. Otherwise they would surely come with her.

"Leah just expressed an interest in your seers, Mr. Johnsson, but I don't know if that would be okay?"

He looked at Leah with a smile. "That's actually perfect. You can compare notes. If you would be so kind to leave them with Gilly. She has quite the knack for making sense of different patterns. I'm sure that includes visions?"

"Yes, sir," Gilly replied immediately.

"In that case, I'd like to tag along with Lee. Kate, do you mind?" Deborah looked at her. Catherine made sure she sent out a wave of calm and reassurance to Deborah. She would feel that.

"I'll be fine. Shame to miss the seers, though. You'll have to tell me all about them later."

"Promise," Leah said with a smile. Peter got up from behind his desk, closing a laptop. "I'll show them the way and guide them back. This can be quite a maze."

"You're not kidding," Catherine heard Leah mumble, as they walked out the door, following his lead. Leah gave her a wave and closed the door behind her.

"Shall we?" Trevor Johnsson motioned her to follow him as well. "Tristan, are you coming?" *Oh, thank God! Would he be allowed to accompany her all the way? Okay, keep it together!* Catherine nodded her consent to Tristan's boss and followed him out the room.

As soon as they had left the room, Trevor set a brisk pace. Catherine had to make an effort to keep up with him. "I'm sure this must be a very weird experience for you, Ms. van Dyk. It is for us, as well. We don't get many civilians in here, as I'm sure you can imagine."

Catherine looked back at Tristan, who was right behind her and gave him a triumphant smile. She'd referred to herself as a civilian once, when Tristan's cover was blown and she had found out why he'd actually been there all the time. Of course, he had laughed at her. It was clear he remembered, because he quickly stuck out his tongue. She hummed her agreement and expressed her gratitude once more.

"Oh no, I didn't mean it like that. If anything, we should be thanking you for still having a life and a job. You did save the world, after all. After you, please?" he motioned for her to step inside a room. She felt confusion coming for Tristan and tried to catch his eye.

"You're really going to give her clearance?" he asked. Catherine thought the room looked like a doctor's office or maybe something from a hospital. There were several big machines.

Trevor looked slightly irritated. "That's what I said, wasn't it? That is, of course, with your permission, Ms. van Dyk. It would make our dealings a lot easier in the next few days and it was actually a request from the big boss upstairs, whom you've met, as I've come to understand it."

A request from her grandmother. Catherine was careful not to mention that little fact. Tristan had explained nobody knew the Serpent's true identity, except for him, her and this William guy. Anybody who ever got to meet the Serpent would be meeting with William.

"Yes, indeed. Most interesting man," she mumbled.

"I couldn't agree more. If you would be so kind, however, to refrain from mentioning his gender from now on. Our employees do not know whether the Serpent is a man or a woman, and we would like to keep it that way. I'm sure you understand. Anonymity is vital in our line of work."

"Of course, I will not mention it again. Is it okay if I just refer to him as the big boss?"

Trevor nodded. "Big boss or the Serpent, both are fine, ma'am. I'll walk you through the procedure. We'll go up after that. The Serpent is expecting you for tea in fifteen minutes."

"Can I accompany her?" Tristan asked his boss. Trevor nodded.

"It was actually requested, so yes." Catherine relaxed the same time she felt Tristan relax. At least they would be together this time. Trevor pointed to a small machine. "This will register your fingerprints. Your right thumb first, please." Catherine pressed down her right thumb. "Good, now all fingers, please?" She had to push down her pinky finger twice, before the machine accepted her prints, but after the second attempt, it flashed green.

"Okay, left hand, same procedure." Making sure to press down her pinky finger, her left hand was accepted at her first attempt. "Excellent. This will give you access to the building. After you've entered your fingerprints, the panel will ask for a five-digit code. You will need it should you be here after hours. You will also need it to access one of the vacant offices to work in."

"Will I be assigned a code?" she asked.

"No, you have to pick one," Tristan replied before Trevor had the chance. "Nothing that anyone would guess, though. So, no birthdays. Not yours or people who are close to you."

Tristan's boss nodded his approval and pointed her to another panel. Both Tristan and Mr. Johnsson took several steps back from her to give her privacy. "You have to enter it twice. Once your name and ID show up on the screen, you've been approved."

Catherine raked her mind. Something that wasn't obvious, but it had to be something she could remember as well. She would hate to ask someone because she forgot her code on her first day here. Suddenly it came to her, perfect. She typed in 21-3-89. The system asked for the same code once more and she retyped. *Eat that, Nana!* It was the date her grandmother had died. Somehow, she found it kind of fitting. After a few seconds, her own face looked back at her, showing her ID. She had to admit, it made her feel very James Bond.

"All done," she said, turning around and stepping away from the machine.

"No retina scan?" Tristan asked. His boss shook his head.

"No, not necessary. We assume she'll never be here unaccompanied, but should the occasion arise, at least she will be able to enter the building without all the fuss."

Catherine saw Tristan nod once shortly.

"Well, welcome to the Company, Ms. van Dyk." Mr. Johnsson gave her a warm smile and gestured for her to follow him. "Now I do believe there is tea waiting for you upstairs, shall we move on?"

Catherine would have liked to take Tristan's hand but decided against it. It was probably not a good idea to let anyone know they were involved. Hadn't he told her that even his relationship with Eve had been frowned upon? They had only allowed it because they had feared the wrath of their only reviver. And as a mind reader, she could do a lot of damage. Catherine kept looking from side to side, taking in as much as she could. Her grandmother had built this company to its current status, after all. It was only natural to be curious. After taking the lift upstairs and turning a few corners, they stopped in front of a large painting. It wasn't like the cornfield, but Catherine swore it could be from the same collection. Ugh, bad memories. She noticed Mr. Johnsson moving forward and had to control herself not to snatch him back. Nothing weird happened, though. The painting didn't bulge, nor was he dragged inside. It seemed to contain a hidden retina scan, and she heard a soft click. The painting swung to the side, revealing another lift.

"Please, get in. Tristan, top floor, if you please. I'm sure you remember. You'll be shown out another way. Ms. van Dyk, it was an absolute pleasure meeting you. This is as far as I go. Have a good flight and most of all, a safe return from New York."

She shook his hand and said, "Thank you, Mr. Johnsson, for your time and hospitality. Also, for giving me clearance to the Company."

He looked at her. "Not my doing, ma'am, but my pleasure.

Tristan," he nodded and stepped back to let the lift doors close.

"Ready?" Tristan asked. She smiled at him.

"Only one way to find out."

The doors opened, revealing a dark hallway. Now this was more like what she had imagined. At the end of the hallway, there was a big double door with silver handles, representing two serpents entwined. The symbol contained a triquetra as well. Catherine smiled and shook her head. Tristan looked at her with some confusion.

"It's our Company logo," he said in a soft voice, probably not wanting to notify anyone on the other side of the doors.

"Is it, now? I should ask for a paycheck. I designed the bloody thing." Catherine noticed he was staring at her.

"Well, I did," she whispered back. "When I was a little girl, I was always sketching. Nana always loved my sketches. I made this one especially for her. My mother had it framed when I was five, and we gave it to her for her birthday. Her last birthday, actually. Next year, the plane crashed. Not that it killed her, obviously. I can't remember seeing it on the building, though. Trust me, I would have noticed."

"It's not. It's only known to Company people. I guess she wanted something of you close by." He motioned for her to do the honours. She knocked and immediately a man's voice responded.

"Enter."

Catherine pulled open one of the doors. Good God, that was one heavy door! Tristan held it for her. She stepped through first and had to squeeze her eyes to adjust to the light. Coming from a dark hallway, this ovular room was extremely bright. Behind her the walls were white, bookcases from top to bottom. The other side was completely made out of glass, though. Looking up, she noticed even the ceiling was made out of glass. There was a big desk in the middle and a seating area on her left. Her grandmother was sitting behind the desk, getting up. A tall man was hovering very close to her. *That must be William then.* She gave him a tentative smile, not sure whether she just act like herself and go hug her grandmother. *Ah, fuck it! To hell with protocol.* She bounced forward and pulled her grandmother in a big hug.

"Hi, Nana, so good to see you again. For real this time. Somehow, a painting doesn't quite count."

Her grandmother looked pleased. "I'm glad you've decided to drop by, my child. Tristan, it is good to see you again. Catherine, may I introduce you to William? William has been my friend and confidante for more than twenty-five years now. And, for all intent and purposes, he is the Serpent. William, my granddaughter, Catherine van Dyk."

"An honour to finally meet the source of your grandmother's inspiration, Ms. van Dyk. I very much hope to get to know you better. I hope you haven't been scared off by Tristan's stories of me?" He smiled at her and even gave Tristan a wink.

Catherine looked at Tristan in confusion. *He wasn't so bad.* He was actually quite nice, as far as she could tell.

"I do apologise, Visconti, but it was quite necessary at the time. We had to be absolutely certain you would do anything for her," William said to him.

Oh, they had been testing Tristan. Well, she probably would have done that herself, right?

William looked at her like she had said something.

Oh right, mind reader, dammit.

"Well, I did imagine you would look like Arnold Schwarzenegger, only the dark-haired version, but you look like a pretty decent man to me. I hope to get to know you better as well. And please, call me Kate. If only to irritate my grandmother. And Tristan, for that matter," she finished with a grin.

Her grandmother rolled her eyes. It was like looking in a mirror. Same expression. How weird to see it again, after all these years. Knowing what she was thinking, William gave her another warm smile.

"Kate, it is. And please, call me William." She nodded.

"Of course, I already know, but how did it go last night? It must have been very hard for you," her grandmother asked.

"It would have been, if Tristan hadn't been there. I was glad to have someone there who was in the know. He actually helped me put a lock on my emotions because honestly, Nana, I think you gave me too much credit. I was really losing it. Oh, and thanks for the collapsed lung."

Her grandmother looked shocked. "Collapsed lung? What are you talking about?"

Tristan frowned as well. "You did not foresee? I thought you must have known Sue would be there to heal her."

"I most certainly did not know. I would never deliberately hurt my granddaughter, Tristan."

Catherine raised an eyebrow. "The jury's is still out on that, Nana. Sorry. And Tristan is telling the truth. I couldn't breathe. Also, I've been worried that the same had happened to you. I'm guessing no then."

"No. William, we will have to look into that. This cannot happen again."

"Of course not. Not to worry. I'll take care of it," he said, and the Serpent seemed convinced.

"Are you okay? You look okay," she asked, looking her up and down.

Catherine sighed. "I'm fine, Grandma. I'm just pointing out there are things you cannot account for, either. And I don't mean to be rude, but I was promised tea."

She saw William trying to hide a smile while her grandmother walked to the seating area. "Of course, where are my manners? Please, do sit down." She poured some hot water in four cups and handed Catherine a box with different flavours. She chose an herbal one with jasmine.

"To answer your question. I am okay. Probably more than I should be. Thankfully Mom and everybody were so worried, they asked very few questions about my time in the painting. Deborah did ask, but I said it was all very blurry. Thankfully, she didn't push it. It's my own guilt that's been eating me alive. I hate keeping secrets from my friends."

Her grandmother looked at her with a speculative look. "William and I have been discussing this. I know you're not me. You are your own person and, therefore, your character is unique. Also, you have not lived my life and are not accustomed to a life of secrecy. Where keeping something a secret can mean the difference between saving someone's life or putting a life on the line. Catherine, I do hope you understand why it's important to not let your mother in on this. As much as I would love to hold her in my arms, it is not to be. It would endanger her life. You will have to trust me on this. However, we've come to the decision you can let Leah and Deborah know who truly runs the Company. Anybody else, will have to deal with either yourself, Tristan, Trevor, or eventually, William. Would that be agreeable to you? Something you can live with?"

She could tell Deb and Lee? That would make a huge difference. Of course, all her other friends popped into her head straight away. In all fairness, though, Leah and Deborah were her lifelong friends. Leah pretty much her whole life, and she couldn't imagine a life without Deborah. And she didn't want to endanger her mother. She and Uncle Ben were all she had left of her close relatives. Tristan knew. William obviously knew. And Roy, Charles, Eve, Alan. Come to think of it, a lot of people already knew her true identity. She realised that must be putting her grandmother at risk as well.

"I think that would help me a lot. I know it's not perfect, but I have to be reasonable here because you've obviously put a lot of thought into this. I do realise you'll be taking a risk. Two more people who know about your existence. And I really appreciate that. I might need your help dealing with Mom or Uncle Ben every now and then. I'm actually most worried about slipping up. What if I make some stupid random comment that will give the whole thing away? Like you said, I was never trained for this sort of thing."

"That's where Tristan comes in or any other empath the Company can provide, though he would be the most obvious choice since your mother knows and trusts him, sort of. Or even Alan. Although I think it's best to keep Alan away from Elizabeth for the foreseeable future. She doesn't like him very much. What I'm trying to say is, we can always do damage control afterwards, though we prefer not to. Interfering with the mind can only be done so many times without consequences."

"Right." Catherine would think about that last comment later on. "When should I tell them?"

"I think it would be best on your way to the airport. You'll be travelling with Charles. It will give them some time to adjust from the shock as well and get their act together before the rest of your friends join you. I would suggest to meet them in person, but my schedule for today is unfortunately very tight and so is yours. What do you know so far about the ball drop event?"

"First time Lee saw it dropping too fast. After the whole asteroid thing, she started to focus on the ball drop. I guess she has been focusing on that so hard, otherwise she would have picked up something about this meeting. Normally, she's very attuned to me and my future."

Her grandmother nodded. "We've been counting on that. I knew she would be focusing on the ball drop. Please, continue."

"Well, more recently she mentioned the ball would explode and inside the ball there seems to be some sort of cloud. Gas, maybe? She's not sure. What she is sure about, is that the surrounding people were killed by the blast of the explosion and she saw a carpet of people, choking to death on the ground. We figured it must be some kind of toxin, or perhaps a virus even."

"It's not a virus," William said, getting up. He walked over to the desk to retrieve a file and gave it to Catherine. "This covers the basics. Tristan, we've uploaded a more detailed file. Kate, you will also be able to read it with your access code. Tristan will provide you with a Company laptop."

"Oh, okay," she said. "What is it then, if not a virus?"

"You were right about the gas part. Sort of, at least. It's a toxin known as botulinum toxin."

Catherine could feel Tristan freeze up next to her.

"You're sure?" Tristan asked, directing his question to William. He nodded.

"Positive, unfortunately. Tristan doesn't like the sound of this and rightfully so, Cathe…excuse me, Kate. He knows it's the most poisonous substance known to mankind."

"Lovely. Who would do such a thing?"

Her grandmother looked at her with a sad expression.

"I wish the answer to that were a simple one and I could say, evil people. Anyone who would be willing to sacrifice this many people, must be stopped. Of that much I'm certain. Of course, it's never that simple and each terrorist organization believes in their cause. Quite passionate, most of the time, which makes them even more dangerous. It's always hard to realise one person's terrorist is another person's hero."

"Which group is it?" Tristan asked.

"This is not one hundred percent confirmed, but we have enough solid leads which points to Aldaw. One of Alan's contacts came through some pretty good intel, which confirmed our own. I spoke to him myself early this morning. This year's ball drop will be quite the event. Ever since September Eleventh, they've been trying to find a way in again for another attack. To them, it would probably be the icing on the cake and they've got at least one man inside."

"Aldaw? I don't think I ever heard of them. Who are they?" Catherine asked.

William looked at her. "It means 'the Light'. They're an Islamic organization and they're not too happy with the current US government. Well, we can't exactly blame them, but still, there are many ways to Rome and theirs is not exactly peaceful. Their motto is kun al-ttaġyira al-a'iī turīdu 'an tarāhu fiī al-'alam."

"Okay. I have no idea what that means," Catherine replied.

"It means be the change you want to see in the world," William said, frowning.

"That doesn't sound so bad," Catherine pondered. "In fact, that could have been something coming from me."

"Mm, yes. You have to ask yourself, though, what kind of change they are looking for and believe me, you will not like the answer. I will show you."

"What would be the first signs the toxin has reached human beings?" Catherine wasn't sure she even wanted to know the answer, but looked at William to respond anyway. He leaned over to turn a page in the file she was holding, and she was instantly horrified. Catherine felt a bit nauseated. She closed the file in front of her, but she could still see the woman and child, both choking to death, eyes bulging.

"Facial paralysis, muscle weakness, trouble swallowing. That's just the beginning. Eventually, it can and will cause heart attacks, seizures, respiratory arrest, or death, depending on how much people breathe in and their own immune system."

"I think that sounds pretty familiar to what Lee saw in her vision," she said, her voice breaking at the end. Tristan slowly rubbed her back.

"Are you okay?"

She nodded. "Yes, I'm fine. It's just a lot to take in. I mean, I love a good spy or action movie, but it's a bit different actually being in one."

"You're doing great, my dear. Truly. My first case, I puked my guts out. I'm not ashamed to admit it." Her grandmother smiled at her.

"Good to hear I have the stomach for terrorism then," she said, a hint of irony in her voice.

"Well, you did defeat a complete asteroid," William said, giving her a wink.

"Somehow, I think I'd take the asteroid again, William. At least, that little fucker had no intention of hurting our planet. It was just on a collision course. These people have been planning this. Probably for years, right?"

"Yes. If you open that file again to the first page, you'll see a picture of Khalil Ahmad Ibrahim Nassar, the current leader of Aldaw. Of course, this is what we think he looks like now, no one knows for sure, as it has been several years since the last real sighting. There's a twenty-five-million-dollar price on his head for any information or intelligence leading to his capture."

Catherine whistled. "Damn, that's a lot of money. Makes you wonder why nobody has turned this guy in. I mean, money corrupts, right?"

"In this case, we hope so. Or at least, the US government hopes so, but it seldom pays off. It is believed he resides somewhere in tribal Pakistan. Last year he gave a speech on video, leaked by Aldaw. Egging people on for another September Eleventh attack. Not only on US soil, but he mentioned European, Israeli, and Russian targets as well. Lovely fellow," William said.

"Has there ever been a botuli…" Catherine opened her file to look at the name of the toxin, but William anticipated her question and answered.

"An attack with botulinum toxin? Actually, yes. The Japanese doomsday cult, Aleph, formerly known as Aum Shinrikyo, produced botulinum toxin and spread it as an aerosol in downtown Tokyo during the nineteen nineties. Thankfully, the attacks caused no fatalities."

"Thank the gods for small favours then. Can it be easily destroyed?" she asked.

Tristan answered this time. "Relatively, yes. It can be destroyed by extreme heat, one hundred and twenty degrees, and at least for thirty minutes. Boiling water would be better, but if it's inside the ball, that will be almost impossible. You'd have to be close to make sure you get everything. We would have to create a sphere of our own."

"At what temperature would the crystals explode?" Catherine asked.

"Crystals can explode, depending on how fast they are heated and depending on the crystal. Hopefully, they can hold one hundred and twenty degrees. We'll get someone on that," Tristan said to her. "Good question, Catherine."

"I have another one. And maybe this is a terribly stupid question, I don't know, but can't we just call the whole thing off, the New Year's ball drop? I mean, I'm sure you have ways of tipping off the NYPD, FBI, CIA, the president for all I care. Wouldn't it be easier to just let them know someone's planning a terrorist attack?"

"That's not a stupid question, Catherine. That is an excellent question. And one we must always keep asking ourselves," her grandmother said to her. "But let me ask you a question in return. Why do you think we haven't done that already?"

"Because this whole company is a secret? Because you know things you aren't supposed to know? Not by surveillance or spy work, but because of what people can do here, because of their gifts?"

Her grandmother smiled. "Well done, my dear. Can you imagine what would happen if the world found out what we can do? We do not answer to the government of the UK. We do not answer to any government. Some suspect, and they are wise enough to keep those suspicions to themselves. No nation would allow a single company this much power, Catherine."

"But couldn't you work around that? I mean, with all your resources, I'm sure it would be a walk in the park for you."

"We could, and sometimes, we do. That's usually when you see an increase in conspiracy theories in the papers and on social media. We have to very careful, Catherine. Which is why we prefer taking matters into our own hands. We're good at what we do. Usually, our way results in the fewest casualties and provides plausible deniability for the appropriate authorities." She looked at the clock.

"We have to get going, right?" Catherine asked Tristan. He nodded. Catherine stood up, stuffing the file in her handbag.

"Have your friend Romy put a glamour on that. Just to be on the safe side," William said to her. For a moment, she didn't understand what he was saying. "In case your handbag gets searched by customs."

"Oh, right! Good thinking. I'll ask her. Nana, will I be able to reach you?"

"Not directly, dear. I'm sorry. William will stay in contact with both of you, though, and should it be necessary, he obviously knows how to reach me. I could contact you in the morning, if you would like that. Your time. It'll be you, Leah and Deborah in her apartment, correct?"

"And Ryan, Leah's partner," Catherine answered automatically.

"No, Ryan's away on business. Didn't Leah tell you?" her grandmother answered.

This took Catherine by surprise. "No, I guess I forgot to ask. I just assumed he would be there. Okay, so relatively safe then. Do you have my number? Silly question, of course you have my number."

Both her grandmother and William smiled.

"Yes, we do, but I won't be calling you on your phone. It will show no caller ID, and I can imagine you might be hesitant to answer such a call away from home. Tristan will provide you with a burner phone. If it rings in the morning, you can be pretty sure it'll be me."

"A burner phone, cool. Do I get to burn it afterwards?" she asked. They all stared at her. "Oh, come on, guys, lighten up! I know what a burner phone is. Jeez, I was just pulling your leg."

"She's your granddaughter, all right," William said to her grandmother, who took a deep breath and sighed.

"Yes, thank you, William." She looked at her granddaughter. "Now, get over here and give your grandmother a hug."

They embraced several seconds. Catherine sniffed her hair, storing the smell in her memory. Pulling back, she took a good look at her. Just a bit taller than she was, same build, though. She looked fragile, only her eyes betrayed the power underneath. Both so very different, yet also the same. She sighed. She would miss her.

"You'll hear from me tomorrow morning, promise," her grandmother said, as if she had read her mind.

"I will keep you updated as often as I can," William said to both Tristan and Catherine. "You keep her safe." William directed this last comment to Tristan.

"With my life, sir."

Catherine's grandmother looked pleased and even William gave him a smile. Catherine sighed.

"Okay, enough with all the damsel in distress stuff. I didn't see any of you stopping an asteroid, okay. I have been known to be able to do a thing or two by myself." She kept her voice light because she was starting to feel a bit emotional again. "Come on, Tristan, we have a plane to catch."

"Yes, ma'am." He pushed the door open for her. Catherine took one last look at her grandmother and William, who both waved goodbye to her. She waved back and blew her grandmother a kiss. Just before the doors closed, she saw her grandmother catching it.

* * *

Leah had been trying to say something at least three times now but failed as soon as she began. Deborah was still rubbing her eyes like she had a terrible headache. Tristan was sitting next to Catherine and Leah and Deborah sat across them in the big company car. Catherine sighed for what felt like the millionth time and was just about to say something, when Leah looked up.

"I can't believe it. I just can't wrap my head around it. What I can say is this. I know this must have a terrible burden for you to keep this from your mother, from us, even for a day, and I want to let you know I don't blame you in the slightest. I definitely don't want to add to that burden."

Deborah stopped rubbing her temples. "God, Kate, that goes for me as well, obviously. I'm so sorry you had to go through this without us. I was just thinking that I'm extremely grateful to you, Tristan, for being there with Kate when we couldn't."

"It was the least I could do. I have to say, Catherine bore it like a champion." He gave her hand a soft squeeze. Leah let out a snorting noise.

"Of course, she did. Didn't you know? Kate is a complete sucker when it comes to self-sacrifice and taking all the heat herself."

Catherine stuck out her tongue to her best friend. "Love you too, honey."

"The important thing, though," Tristan said to all of them. "is that you have to keep this to yourself. You can only talk about this at Leah's home and only when it is just you three. That means no Romy, no Meg, no Sue. I know this is asking a lot and frankly, when you're not used to keeping secrets, I find it easiest when you do not discuss it at all. At least not for a while. Focus on the case at hand and when necessary refer to Catherine's grandmother as the big boss or the Serpent."

Catherine heard Deborah exhale in a huff. "Oh man, this is going to be a disaster. There's a reason why we're never able to throw each other a surprise party. We suck at keeping secrets, Tristan. You couldn't have picked a lousier trinity than us three." Deborah raised her hands in the air as if she we're saying, just shoot me.

Catherine had to laugh. "I told him as much, but he has faith in us. The Serpent has faith in us." Saying it felt strange, but it also created a bit of a distance, which she needed right now. It did help to see it a bit more objectively. "We'll be arriving at the airport soon and everybody will be there. The guys as well. We can only assume they'll be full of questions, too."

Leah nodded. "I did try to explain best I could last night, but honestly, there wasn't a lot to explain. Sue knows first-hand the shape you were in, of course, but we didn't have much to go on. I got a text from her this morning asking me how you we're feeling. I told her you were completely healed, back to your normal self, but you still didn't remember anything other than a big blur."

Catherine sighed. "Okay, that's good, I can deal with that. Thanks, Lee."

"You're welcome," she replied. "How are we going to tell them about the whole terrorist attack? Should we even involve them? I mean, this was supposed to be a fun outing. I think Harry and Martin still haven't recovered from our latest stunt."

Tristan cleared his throat. "I think, at the very least, you will have to notify them about what will happen at the ball drop. They must be given a choice to stay away from the area. If they're nowhere near Times Square, they should be fine, but it has to be their choice. Leah, you got them all tickets for New Year's Eve, right?"

She nodded. "Yes, the best money could buy. At the New York Knickerbocker Hotel. They have the best view. We even have our own Skybox. Don't ask. I've been there before. It's actually really good, thought I doubt we're going to be there, right?"

"That's yet to be decided," Tristan replied. "If it's up to us, we get that ball decontaminated before the actual drop. We have to consider worst case scenario, though. In that case, I would not recommend the Knickerbocker. It's too close."

"Right. Oh well, it's only money." Leah shrugged.

"The Company can cover any costs you make, Leah. That goes

for all of you." Tristan looked at Deborah and Catherine as well.

"Don't be silly," Leah said. "I made those reservations months ago, just before Samhuinn. Who knows? We might get lucky."

"At least you know the option is there," Tristan said. "Is there anything you want to get off your chest, ladies? Because now is your chance."

"Are you coming with us?" Deborah asked. "On the plane, I mean?"

"Yes and no," Tristan replied. "We're flying to New York as well, but we're flying a Company plane. We thought it would be too much of a hassle to book first class on the same plane and let you deal with a lot of explaining to the rest of the party. No, we'll drop you off and we'll be there when you land. Our planes are a bit faster."

"Where will you stay?" Catherine asked.

"We own several places there. I'll be there as soon as I can, honey. Promise."

Leah was going through her purse. "If you're really there before we arrive, why don't you go to my place? I really don't mind, as long as we're sure you'll be there. I don't feel like sitting in front of my own apartment, but other than that, you're welcome to hang out at my place." She handed him a set of keys.

"That's awfully kind, Leah. Are you sure? Like I said, we have plenty of options."

She shook her head. "No, I know that. And as much as you would be welcome to stay, I actually don't have any more room for overnight guests. I just thought it would be handy to meet at my place. This way you don't have to wait until we get there and do whatever it is you do, and Kate doesn't have to wait any longer than necessary to see you."

Catherine smiled at her. Leah knew her so well.

"Then, thank you, Leah," Tristan said, accepting the keys. "I'll keep these safe."

"You better," she said but smiled nonetheless. "And Tristan, please feel free to consider my home your home, okay? If you, or Roy or Charles want anything to drink or eat, please, help yourselves."

"Thank you, Leah. We really appreciate it. If that's okay with the three of you, I would like to invite Alan and Eve over as soon as possible. Catherine wants to speak to Alan and I thought you said you wanted to meet Eve as well, right?" He looked at her.

"Yes, if anything, to thank her for saving my life. And I really need to talk to Alan. Besides, we're going to work together. Better to get acquainted, or in Alan's case, re-acquainted. We don't have that many days left. God, Deja-vu. Why is it we're always cutting this crap so close?"

"Welcome to my world," Tristan said. The car pulled up at the airport and Charles got out to get their bags.

"Thank you, Charles, I'll see you soon then," Catherine said to the older man and gave him a hug. He looked embarrassed but very pleased nonetheless.

"Looking forward to it, Miss Catherine. Ladies," He tapped his hat and gave Tristan some space to say goodbye. Leah and Deborah pretended to be interested in the flight schedule to give them some privacy.

"It's just the flight, and you have Leah and Deborah by your side. Do you need me to calm you or are you okay?" he asked with concern.

She shook her head and smiled at him.

"No, I'm okay. Really, I feel much better now that Lee and Deb are in the know. It helps. I might even be able to pull this off. Take care of my heart. I'm leaving it with you."

Tristan smiled. "I'll protect it with my soul. Come get it back as soon as you can. Love you," he said before gently kissing her lips.

"Love you more," she replied, giving him one last hug. "Okay, ladies, ready to face our demons? Uhm, friends. I mean friends. Did I say demons?" Catherine said, which made them all laugh as they walked into Heathrow Airport.

Eve

"Eve, for the love of God, will you stop fidgeting? You're making me nervous, for crying out loud!" Roy looked at her like she had just gone completely mad.

"They're still at least fifteen minutes out. Give it a rest. They're not going to bite your head off."

"Shut up, Roy. I know that," Eve said, tossing her hair over her shoulder. "I just think it's important that we all get along. I'm still not sure we should be here when they arrive. It's Leah's home, after all. We might not be welcome."

Tristan sighed. "I've already discussed this with Leah, like I told you ten minutes ago. They know we wanted to get you over here as soon as possible anyway. Best to get it out of the way immediately, right?"

"Fine," she snapped. She looked at Alan, who had been awfully quiet and at ease since the minute they'd arrived at Leah's home. It irritated her. He could at least have the decency to feel a little nervous as well. Apparently, nothing seemed to be bothering Alan. He'd even been civil to Tristan, so far. He was currently flipping through Leah's stack of newspapers, catching up with the local news as he had commented when she asked him why the hell he was wasting his time with going through a stack of old newspapers.

"Well, if they're only fifteen minutes away, I'm coming to make a pot of coffee. I'm sure they will like something real after the rubbish they serve on the plane." Eve left for the kitchen to look for a coffeemaker. Leah appeared to be an old-fashioned kind of woman when it came to making coffee. Eve found a filter coffee machine and smiled. Just the way she liked it. There was a grinder as well, and Eve chose a dark roast coffee bean. She filled the coffeemaker with water and pressed the on switch. After a few seconds, the coffeemaker started to rumble. She loved that sound and closed her eyes for a moment.

Yes, calm. That was it. Eve wasn't sure why she was feeling nervous. She guessed it was the whole Alan-Tristan situation. Tristan had been her former lover, like Alan had been Catherine's. To be honest, it was kind of a weird situation. However, she was sure Catherine would be feeling the same way. Plus, she just had the fact her grandmother was still alive dumped on her and had pretty much been told to deal with it as soon as possible, so all things considered, Eve had to admit she was probably in the better position here.

"They're here!" Eve heard Roy shout from the living room and sighed.

Come on, woman. People are supposed to be scared of you, not the other way around.

Eve pulled herself together and walked back into the living room. She could hear noises at the front door and three women, a bit worse for wear, came walking into the living room. She picked out Catherine easily, having seen her in real life before. Leah was the tall blonde and Deborah managed to look like she'd just been on a fifteen-minute bus ride instead of an eight-hour flight. Only her eyes betrayed her fatigue.

So, this is Eve. Christ, she is beautiful. No wonder Tristan fell for her. Eve stared at Catherine, both shocked and pleased to hear Catherine think these words, but trying very hard not to listen to anything else inside her mind. It was just too awkward. She realised Tristan was about to say something, but she beat him to the punch.

"Leah, please forgive us for invading your home uninvited. Tristan thought it best to meet as soon as possible. I hope you don't mind the intrusion. You all must be very tired. I know Alan and I are both jet-lagged." Eve took a step towards Leah to give her a hand, which Leah took.

"It's not a problem, Eve. Please don't make yourself uncomfortable. I saw on the plane you two would be here, so we were
expecting you. It is nice to finally meet you. Also, thank you for
saving my friend's life. We owe you a great deal."

"Thank you, Leah. That is very gracious of you. You don't owe
me anything, though. None of you do." She looked at Deborah
and finally at Catherine. The latter was having a hard time keeping
it together. Seeing Alan had stirred up a big chunk of guilt, and
Eve couldn't help but feeling sorry for her.

"I'm sure you two would like to talk," she said to her with a smile.

Catherine gave her a hesitant smile in return. "It's nice to meet
you, Eve. I know you see it differently, but I am very grateful to
you for saving my life. Please, just let me say that. If there's ever
anything I can do for you, I hope you will feel free to ask."

Eve decided not to make a big deal out of this. Obviously, it
made the woman feel better. Why deny her that? "Well then, I
guess, my pleasure?" She shook the hand Catherine held out to
her. She shook Deborah's hand as well.

"Who made coffee?" Leah asked, sniffing the air.

"I did," Eve replied. "I thought you'd like a good cup of coffee
instead of the poor substitute they provide on the plane."

"Oh, thank fuck!" Leah said. "I like her already," she said to
Tristan, who smiled. "Roy, come and make yourself useful for a
change and help me in the kitchen." Leah walked to the kitchen,
not even waiting to see if Roy would follow. "Oh, and Alan, be
a dear, and don't ruin the order of my newspapers," she said over
her shoulder.

Eve noticed Alan's surprise at Leah's relaxed, almost teasing
response. She knew Leah had been the only one of Catherine's
friends he knew well and even got along with just fine. They had
been friends back in the Netherlands. That had all changed, of
course, after he and Catherine had broken up. He'd never blamed
her for choosing Catherine' side, he would have done the same

thing, but he had confessed to her he was hoping to restore their former friendship. Eve focused on Leah's thoughts and found nothing bit sincerity before she walked out of range towards the kitchen. She smiled and nodded at Alan to let him know Leah was not playing games with him. Apparently, she was dead-set on giving Alan a second chance. Eve had a feeling she herself would get along with Leah just fine.

Alan grinned. "Wouldn't dream of it. Nice to see you too, Leah."

Alan was looking at her. *Should I approach her? What do you think?* he was saying in his mind. Eve gave him a short nod, which went unnoticed by the rest.

"Hey, Cat," he said to Catherine, "dit had je een jaar geleden vast niet kunnen bedenken." He gave her a gentle smile.

Catherine let out a nervous laugh. "Understatement of the year, Alan. Je ziet er goed uit."

She noticed Catherine's lower lip began to tremble. Eve looked at both Alan and Tristan. *A bit of help for this woman, please.* God, empaths could be so stupid sometimes!

Eve was only able to understand what was in people's minds. In their minds, language apparently worked on a universal level, she had as little difficulty understanding the thoughts of a British person than she would a Chinese person. When they were speaking out loud, though, not so much. Then she had to understand the actual language, and Eve had never learned how to speak Dutch. She had visited the Netherlands on many occasions, but the Dutch were all fluent in the English language. It had never been necessary. She was wondering what they both had said to each other.

Alan leaned over Catherine, his hands on either side of her cheeks. She could hear Tristan moving a step closer and hoped he would keep it together.

"Hey, look at me. Cat, kijk me eens aan. Ik vergeef het je, oke. It was a stupid accident. We'll talk about it later, okay? And let's be honest, I gave you plenty of reason to doubt me." He pulled her into an embrace. Behind her, Eve could hear Tristan gritting his teeth, but he did not intervene.

Catherine slowly pulled back, wiping away the tears in her eyes and gave him a watery smile. On cue, Roy and Leah came back in, both holding up a tray with cups, coffee, sugar, milk and cookies.

"Oh lovely, Alan. I leave the room for one single minute and you have her crying her eyes out. Some empath!" Leah said in a huff.

"What did I do? I swear I was on my best behaviour. Cat, back me up here."

Catherine nodded, trying to pull herself together. "He was, Lee. It's just me. My emotions are all over the place. Normally I'm more of a together person, Eve. I'm sorry you have to see me like this."

Eve gave her a reassuring smile. "Not at all. You've been under a lot of stress lately. It's only natural. However, with two empaths present, I have been wondering why neither of them felt compelled to calm your nerves." The last comment she directed to both Alan and Tristan with just a touch of venom. Both men looked guilty immediately.

"I'll do it," Tristan said before Alan could say anything. Alan rolled his eyes towards Eve but said nothing.

"En toen was er…," he mumbled.

"Koffie," Leah, Catherine and Deborah replied simultaneously. They all started to laugh. Catherine perhaps the most, when she saw the look on Tristan's face.

"It's a Dutch saying, hon. Well, not even that, actually. It's from a very old commercial. We do love our coffee, and Douwe Egberts is really big in our country. It means, time for coffee, time to relax, have a moment for yourself. Everybody knows it, young and old. Ohh, it feels good to laugh. I needed that."

The atmosphere in the room had lightened up, even though Eve could tell Tristan wasn't too happy about Catherine and Alan sharing memories. Well, tough titty. He would just have to suck it up.

"How was your flight, by the way?" she asked the ladies in general.

Catherine replied. "Not too shabby. Business class really helps. I remember the time when I still travelled coach. This is so much better. And I finally got to see the new James Bond movie. I still hadn't got around to it."

"Oh, did you watch that as well?" Deborah replied. "I turned it on to shut out Meg. She kept nagging me and giving me the third degree. Just because I suggested this didn't have to be their fight. That we would not hold it against them for sitting this one out. Like I was holding back information, or something. Well, I was, of course, but still. Good God, that woman's tenacious. Like a dog with a bone. Good movie, though."

"You, Leah?" Eve asked her.

"I watched some reruns of the *X-Files*. I also tried to focus on that idiot in Kate's file, but so far, I'm coming up diddly squat."

Tristan was looking at Deborah. "Was Meg giving you a hard time? Did you have time to explain anything on the plane?"

Leah answered in Deborah's place. "We did get a chance to explain some things, yes. Regular bathroom breaks, stretching your legs, and all. We kept Harry and Martin out of the conversation. It's up to them whether or not they want to be involved. We also tried to explain this by no means obligated them to work with us on this, but we decided it would be wise to drop that really quick. You see, that was what Meg was nagging Deb here about. Every time Harry went to stretch his legs, she would jump on poor Deb saying she couldn't believe we had actually suggested to leave them out of this. We really annoyed the crap out of her. The only thing she did comment on was that she would be out as soon as she would see a grey mist around everyone."

"Meg saw a grey mist? Like an actual grey mist? Or more like something she alone could see? When did she see that?" Alan sounded really interested.

"Back when the asteroid was hanging over our heads, so to speak. She saw it more clearly around me, but when she focused, she realised she saw it around everybody," Catherine answered him.

"Hmm, interesting. I would very much like to meet her." He emptied his cup and poured himself a refill. "Anyone else?" A few people nodded.

"Why is that interesting, Alan?" Roy asked him, turning away from his laptop. Eve wondered if that man ever stopped working. Roy had been behind his laptop almost the moment he came back from the kitchen with Leah.

"Because it's what I see. The grey mist, I mean. It's the potential of death. Let's face it, if there's one thing sure in this life, it's we're all going to die sometime. It becomes clearer when someone is sick or in danger. She has the makings of becoming a master of death. I told Eve as much. That's why I'm saying, I would very much like to meet her. I've never met anyone with the same potential."

"Oh! Well, that's uhm. Wow, I really don't know how to respond to that. You will have to take it up with Meg yourself. She's always been convinced she could only see death. That's all I can tell you, right?" Catherine said to him, looking at both her friends for support.

Deborah shrugged. "To be honest, I always doubted that she wouldn't be able to do more. I think it has more to do with intent and knowing how to unlock your own potential. I've been meaning to thank you for that, Tristan. You really helped me enhance my powers."

Tristan smiled at her. "That makes me very happy, Deborah. I'm glad I could be of assistance."

"Your powers have increased, quite substantially even," Alan said, staring at her. "As I'm sure Kate has told you, I can also sense people's potential. Though we've never been properly acquainted with one another, our paths did cross several times back in Holland. Your powers weren't nearly as developed as they are now."

"Oh. Well, I'm glad to hear my efforts are paying off then." Deborah answered, her cheeks, a bit flushed. For someone who put so much effort in looking her absolute best, Deborah didn't like to be in the spotlight.

Eve could easily make out her thoughts. She turned her head when she picked up something in Catherine's mind.

"Please, just ask, Catherine," she said to her.

Catherine flushed red. "Oh, I'm sorry. I was just curious. Well, I was thinking, Alan is not only a master of death. He can also hurt people. Like give them a headache or something. No offense, Alan. Just telling it like it is."

He shrugged. "None taken."

"You are a reviver. Does that mean you can also heal people? Like Sue or Deborah?"

"The simple answer is yes. It's a bit more complex than that, though. Like with Alan's power, the most extreme is the one that comes naturally. In my case, reviving. The subtler art of healing came later. I did have an advantage over my fellow healers, though. I'm also a mind reader. Have been all my life. It helps when you can actually hear where it hurts, so I qualified as a healer pretty quick. They seldom use that aspect of my powers, though. We have plenty of healers at the Company."

"Wow. You have to be qualified? Like take a test or something?" Leah asked.

"Oh, yes. Actually, we have them every year. Or whenever we get hurt. You have to be cleared for duty, you see."

"Right. Of course, cleared for duty," Leah said, trying to look knowledgeable. Both Catherine and Deborah were trying to hide a snigger. "Oh what? Like you two are experts on all things spy and shit?" That made the whole room laugh.

"Are you meeting the rest for dinner?" Tristan asked.

Leah nodded. "That is indeed the plan. We'll be trying to make it at least till nine p.m., otherwise we'll be sure to lie awake all night."

Alan snorted. "Trust me, that'll happen anyway. We stayed up till after midnight and even then, I woke up at three-thirty. Bloody annoying."

Leah shrugged. "Yeah, I know. It sucks. Worst thing is, you won't be here long enough to really get used to it."

"Oh, I don't know, Leah. I've taken quite a fancy to New York. I might stick around for a while. I guess that also depends on what the Company decides to do. Eve and I are both still wanted people, after all," Alan said to her.

"Not if I can help it," Catherine hissed. "She owes me big time, and she knows it. If necessary, I'll play up the guilt trip. The very least I can do for the both of you is give you back your freedom."

"Serpent, Catherine. Serpent," Tristan gently reminded her.

She waved her hand in irritation. "Yes, whatever. We're all in the know here, right? I'll be careful outside of this company. Pun totally intended."

Eve gave Tristan an evil grin. "Good luck with this one, Tristan. You do know how to pick them. And I thought I was a handful. Ha ha." She winked at Catherine.

Tristan, however, did not take the bait. "Right back at ya!"

Alan pretended to look affronted. "Hey, who are you calling a handful?"

"Anyway," Leah continued, "I assume you'll not be joining our party? Because if you are, I have to adjust the reservation. You are welcome to join us. It's just that when I made the reservation, I didn't know our group would be a tad larger. And how large is large, come to think of it? I haven't seen Charles around."

"No, we left Charles in Coney Island to arrange things for us with the team we flew in. The Company has an office there. We were there last night. He's setting things up with Peter, Roy's second-in-command."

"Yes, we met Peter and Gilly this morning. That was this morning, right?" Leah frowned.

Eve smiled. "Yes, London time. Anyway, like I said, there are a few others as well who came along with Tristan's team on the plane. Basically, the usual crew. A few snipers, a freezer, a shape shifter and we've pretty much got the rest covered amongst the rest of us right here."

"Wow, back up!" Leah said. "What's that about a freezer and all?"

"Oh, sorry, I'm never sure what Tristan has or has not explained to you. A freezer is someone with the ability to slow down time. They can literally freeze a room full of people, trapped in time. Depending on the capacity of their powers, it only lasts for a couple of seconds. However, it can give you a few much needed seconds to dodge a bullet or defuse a bomb."

"Uh-huh. Sure. Sure, defusing bombs, very important. I'm trying to act blasé about this, so please continue, before I totally give myself away," Leah said. Catherine and Deborah were hanging onto every word Eve was saying as well.

"Okay, I'll pretend not to notice. Nice job, by the way, you almost had me fooled. So, a shape shifter is pretty much self-explanatory, I would think. He or she can take on any human form they want. It's way better than a glamour. There are ways to disarm a glamour, if you know there's a glamour in place. A shape shifter only changes back to its true form when killed. Or, of course, by their own choice, which is far less harmful than being killed."

"That's one nifty power. I don't think we've ever met one, have we?" Deborah asked, her question directed at both Leah and Catherine.

"Well, how would we know? It could have been anybody, but let's go with no." Catherine replied. "A blocker is someone like Charles, right? Or… or William."

Eve narrowed her eyes. "Yes. I know William quite well, actually. He practically raised me. And until recently, I did believe he was the Serpent. His gift is the only one I can't protrude, you see. A good blocker can block pretty much anything. It must have been very easy for him to keep those thoughts to himself. I never suspected anything. I always thought Charles had the potential to be his successor, but I guess the Serpent has different plans for him."

"You did not mention a seer on the team you flew in. You don't need one?" Leah asked.

Eve shrugged. "Why would we? We have you, don't we? In my book, that's way better than the famous four."

Eve could hear Leah's confusion, but before she could elaborate, Tristan answered Leah's unspoken question.

"Eve is not a fan of the Company seers, the Serpent withstanding. But mainly she thinks they are highly overrated. And even I have to admit, they are a bit weird."

"Oh, thank God, I thought it was just us," Deborah cried out. "I swear, I thought we had ended up in the movie *Minority Report*. Have you seen that one, with Tom Cruise? They have these three Precogs who lie in the water in a creepy sort of way. They can hardly function outside of the water. Anyway, we were…umm… sort of reminded of that when we met your seers. They're not really 'here', are they? Or are they on drugs?"

Eve laughed out loud and couldn't stop for a full minute. She actually felt tears in her eyes from the laughter. "Ooh my, that felt good. I am sorry for the rudeness, but your reaction was priceless. I'm glad someone else is seeing it my way, though. I can assure you, they are not on drugs. They're all just naturally weird. I do hope they could give you some useful information. The Company pays those women a lot of money. Come to think of it, I don't think I ever met a male seer."

"I would love to hear more about all the different abilities you've come across at the Company, but we digress from my original question. Are you all going to join us for dinner?" Leah asked.

Eve looked at Tristan.

"I'm not sure that would be a good idea, Leah," Tristan replied. "Besides, we have to debrief our own team members as well."

"Peter can do that, boss," Roy said, turning his attention away from his laptop. "Charles is almost done anyway."

"Besides, sharing food connects people, right? It would be a good opportunity to get to know each other a little better, won't it?" Deborah said.

"So, plus five?" Leah asked. "Tristan, Roy, Charles, Eve and Alan?"

"You're all sure about this? No reservations?" Tristan asked. Nobody commented.

"Plus five it is. I'll call them straightaway." She picked up her phone from the table and put her words into action. "Hello, this is Leah Winter speaking. I have a reservation at six p.m. for eight people. Yes, indeed. No, I do not wish to cancel. I'd like to add five more people to our party, if that's okay?" She was silent for a moment. "Perfect, yes I know where that is. Thank you so much for your trouble. Until tonight then." She put her phone down again.

"All set. They have a small parlour to the side with two tables, just for our group, so we'll have plenty of privacy. And, on the subject of getting to know each other, we could switch tables with each course."

"Oh goody, like speed dating," Alan said, a light teasing in his voice. Eve saw Catherine roll her eyes at him.

"Other than dinner, do we have any plans for today? I mean, how fast does your company usually move?" Leah asked, ignoring Alan's little jab.

"Pretty fast. We have to because we're working under a limited time frame here, considering today's December twenty nine already. Preferably, we would dismantle the ball tomorrow. That would be our best-case scenario. We would need Catherine for that, obviously, to contain the toxin inside, but we still have no idea how many people they have on the inside. I can stop most people, but I can't see everything coming. At least, I'm not willing to take that risk."

"So, you'd like to have me there as well?" Alan asked. Tristan gave him a short nod. "Consider me there," he replied.

"Then, if one of you screws up, my services could come in handy, so I guess I'm tagging along for the ride as well. What will our cover be?" Eve asked.

"That's the tricky part," Roy said. "It won't be easy to get up there the day before New Year's Eve. Not without some serious glamouring or shape shifting skills."

"Or mind control," Alan chipped in. "And before you get all high and mighty, Tristan…I just want to point out there's really not much difference between a glamour, making someone believe what they're seeing or putting the thoughts in their minds. Eve and I used it yesterday for our visit to the Times Square Alliance. We posed as NYPD officers with the uniform and all, but it made our job a lot easier. I'm just saying."

"Duly noted. Thank you, Alan. I'm not against mind control, but I'm just not a fan, either. You know it can cause permanent damage."

Alan rolled his eyes. "Oh please. Come on, Tristan. Only if done incorrectly, and I'm sure you're the extremely careful type anyway, so little chance of that happening. If, however, you'd feel more comfortable with me doing the actual mind control, you know I don't have any problems with that."

"I'm sure I'll manage, thank you," Tristan replied coolly.

"Well, if you two are done comparing the size of your penises, can we get back to the issue at hand? How we're going to get up there?" Catherine blurted out.

Eve discretely turned away, so nobody saw her laugh. *Oh my God, she's really something.*

"I'm sorry, Cat. You know I didn't mean anything by it," Alan said in a gentle voice. Eve automatically focused on his mind but couldn't find any ulterior motive in his thoughts. Alan really did not want to pick a fight with Tristan. It was more that sometimes he couldn't help himself. In a way, they we're so much alike, yet so very different.

"Is there anything Deborah and I can do?" Leah asked.

"We've been thinking about that as well." Alan replied. "Besides trying to see anything that could help us catch these assholes, we were thinking of using Lee's fame to get us up there. Maybe even enhanced by Deborah's powers of persuasion. Also, we thought Deborah might actually know some of the artists performing and could work her way in to provide her assistance for their well-being?"

"Oh!" Deborah exclaimed, looking at Leah. "Well, I'm not sure I can be that persuasive, to be honest, but I can certainly look at the list and see if anybody sounds familiar. Lee, do you think you could get us in?"

Leah pulled her hand through her hair. "Wow, that's a pretty tall order, you guys. Don't get me wrong, I have no scruples whatsoever using my name to get you in, but this is the Times Square ball drop we're talking about. If it had been last week, before Christmas, then maybe. But tomorrow? I really don't think so. Having said that, can't hurt to try, right?"

"That's not entirely true," Roy said, once more abandoning his laptop. "If we go with that particular plan, they will have your name. Anything that might happen to the ball on that same day, you can bet for sure the NYPD will be knocking on your door before you can blink. If only to get you in for questioning and that's best-case scenario."

"Ooh, right. Suddenly I'm not liking this plan so much. Sorry Alan, it was a good idea." Leah said to him.

He shrugged. "Hey, it was worth a try. Desperate times call for desperate measures. We never said we should go with this. It was just something we thought up. So, could we use the shape shifter?"

"I'm leaning towards shape shifter as well," Tristan said.

"Yep, me too!" Roy called from behind his laptop.

"Who would the shape shifter represent?" Catherine asked.

Eve shrugged. "Anyone with authority always works. We could pose as NYPD again, say we're there to do a final check. Marcus can shape shift into the chief inspector or something, and we could tag along."

"So, Marcus is a he then? The shape shifter?" Leah asked.

Eve smiled.

"Yes, a very pretty young man from the island of Jamaica. He's been quite an asset to the Company." Eve felt Alan's eyes on her and smiled. "Not as pretty as you, my love."

Roy made a gagging noise from the other side of the room. Eve picked a lump of sugar from the bowl and threw it with perfect accuracy at his head.

"Ouch! That hurt, Eve."

"Hopefully, it will teach you some manners. Charles would have wacked you over the head, and you know it. To continue, though, Marcus is just one of the team members Tristan flew in. Actually, we have Marcus, who is a shape shifter and very pretty, as I mentioned before and Igor. He's our top freezer and he's massive. I'm not kidding. Igor's from Russia, and he's almost seven feet tall, there's no going around him. He's very friendly, though, like a bear. Only the cuddly kind, not the rip your throat out kind."

"Okay, so what have we got so far?" Leah asked. "Dammit, where is Gilly when you need her? That woman has some serious planning skills."

"Don't worry, Leah, anything you say, is going straight to my team. What do you think I've been doing this entire time?" Roy said, typing away at double speed.

"Oh, that's great. Hopefully, she'll come up with something that actually makes sense. As I was saying, tonight we're having dinner together," Leah said. "Well, I say tonight, that would be in half an hour. Time has been moving quickly. We'll fill in the rest of our group, get everything back to...whose team is it anyway?" Eve, Roy and Alan all pointed at Tristan. "Tristan's team then and take it from there. I dare say we also need our wits about us, so a good night's sleep seems important. After dinner, is there anything we still need to do before everyone can return to their own sleeping arrangements?"

"Unless something unexpected comes up, which you would probably know best, I don't think so." Tristan said to her. "Okay then, time to get something to eat."

Eve raised her hand. "Uhm, about that, I'm a pretty good mind reader, but I didn't catch the name of the restaurant, Leah."

"Oh gosh, how stupid of me! Of course. Here, I'll write down the address for you. It's a Japanese restaurant, by the way. I hope that's okay with all of you. Nobody has any allergies to seafood?"

"I can speak for all of them, Leah. Everybody here loves Asian food," Eve said to her and gave her a smile.

"Good, that's one less thing to worry about. It's called Ginza Onodera. They're located at Four Sixty-One Fifth Avenue. Dinner's on me by the way. We're celebrating the filming of my book."

"The Company pays for all expenses, Leah. Serpent's orders," Tristan said. Leah was about to protest when he cut her off. "Hey, don't shoot the messenger. Take it up with the Serpent when you're back."

She shrugged. "Fine, whatever. God, Kate, does being obnoxious and stubborn as hell run in the family?"

"What did I do?" Catherine exclaimed. "Like he said, take it up with the Serpent, Lee." She stuck out her tongue.

"Are you here by car of by public transport?" Leah asked.

"Roy and I came by car." Tristan said.

"Alan and I are both parked outside. Do you know if there's a parking space for bikes close by?"

"I'm sorry. I'm not sure about that, Eve. I always use public transport myself or grab a yellow cab. I never pay attention to any parking garages."

"Already searching," Roy said from behind his screen. Once they had found a spot, everybody started packing their things.

"Oh dear, I didn't even take a shower or have a chance to change clothes," Deborah whined.

Catherine gave her a friendly slap on the shoulder. "Oh, Deb, you still look amazing. Don't you worry about it. Tonight, you can crash and soak as long as you. I'll even give you the big en suite bathroom, the one with the bathtub."

"Ahh, thanks, Kate, that's really sweet of you."

"Not sure if I can be that persuasive, my ass," Alan mumbled. Deborah looked affronted, but both Catherine and Leah laughed at Alan's comment.

Eve smiled as well. Today had proved very interesting, so far. And they had yet to meet Romy, Sue and Meg. She grabbed her jacket and helmet and followed them down the hallway and out the door.

Tristan

The first fifteen minutes had been kind of awkward. Especially since Leah hadn't bothered to give the others advance notice there would be an addition to their party. Tristan had made sure everybody was in a peaceful mood. Alan had joined in as well. He had felt it. Of course, the tension was mostly addressed to Alan and Eve, so he'd obviously felt inclined to do his bit. Tristan sighed. He knew he would have to let go of this grudge he felt towards Alan. In all fairness, he did seem to do his best, and Tristan could no longer doubt he had true feelings for Eve, having felt them himself.

Ginza Onodera was indeed a Japanese restaurant. In fact, they even had a Michelin star, which reflected on the prices of the menu. At least, they didn't have to go through the process of letting everyone choose something. Ginza Onodera worked with a tasting menu only. They had picked the perfect spot. It was a nice, secluded area, separated with bamboo screens. Their corner held two tables, one for seven people and one for six. Catherine had gone through great lengths to get everybody mixed up, but it had turned out okay on its own. Meg seemed very interested to get to know Alan, and so Harry ended up at his table as well. Catherine was still standing, talking to everybody, currently hugging Sue.

Eve had taken a shine to Leah. The two women were talking animatedly about the pros and cons of seeing what people would do or to hear them think it. Roy had practically cornered Deborah to make sure he could sit next to her. Charles, always the gentleman, was engaging Romy and Martin in a conversation when their drinks arrived.

Leah raised her glass when everybody was seated. "I'm very

happy to share this moment with you. All of you. Now, our Catherine has been made an offer to work for, or at least with, Tristan's company, which is also the reason why our party has expanded. As if her life wasn't exciting enough as it is." They all laughed. "No, Kate, honestly, whatever you decide, we'll back you up all the way. Unfortunately, there's no rest for the wicked, so I'm afraid the next couple of days aren't all going to be about Central Park and caramel apples, which is, a sad, sad announcement. I am well aware. Tonight, let's celebrate old friendships, re-establish former friendships and create new ones. Cin cin!"

They all raised their glasses.

Catherine stood up. "Thank you, Leah, for stepping so graciously away from the limelight, but you're not going to get away with that, as I'm sure you could have foreseen. Something extraordinary has happened and we are so extremely proud of you. We never had any doubt, of course, that you would make it big, but to see *Frozen* on the big screen next year is beyond your wildest dreams and we are so, so happy for you." Catherine stopped to grab something from the table next to her. "And so, what to give the woman who has it all and can certainly see what you're going to get her for each bloody birthday?" They all laughed again. "However, we were betting on you being too focused on this little trip that this would come as a surprise."

"I have no freaking clue, you silly people," Leah said, her voice a bit choked up from emotions. "Thank you." She gave Catherine a hug.

"Do I have to open it now?"

"Yes!" everybody replied. Leah started to unwrap the giftwrapping. It revealed a big wooden, director's clapboard. The director's name was added and under his name was another line which said: *Author: Leah Winter*. The date showed the first date of filming, scene 1, take 1.

"Aww, you guys, this is so cool! I really had no idea. Thank you so much, this is going to get a place of honour in my home. And

I'm definitely bringing this puppy to the set at least once."

The first tasting arrived, and they all sat down while the chef himself came to explain what was what, no doubt pleased they had a famous author in their establishment. They thanked him. Leah stood up again, taking pictures here and there. Tristan smiled when she passed his table and gave his shoulder a squeeze. He had joined Romy, Martin, Deborah, Roy, Eve and Sue. Next to him at the other table Leah was just snapping a picture of Catherine and Alan. He heard her say "for old times' sake." They both rolled their eyes at her but smiled for the picture nonetheless. Alan turned his attention back to Meg and Harry. Charles pulled a chair back for Leah, so she could sit down as well and asked if he could see the clapboard up close. Catherine was leaning in to take a closer look as well.

At Tristan's table, Eve was engaging Sue in a conversation about healing. Tristan tried to focus on the conversation, but his eyes kept slipping towards Catherine. For someone who had been on an eight-hour flight, with no time to change clothes and having quite an emotional morning, he thought she still looked amazing. He greatly admired how she was handling all of this. Part of it was probably gratitude. She was so happy to have her grandmother back in her life. She would have pretty much dealt with anything, including becoming a part of the Company. Tristan had a feeling the Serpent and William had been betting on that. Also, with William not using his blocking powers to shield Catherine's grandmother, he knew there was something she wasn't telling her granddaughter. He had felt it but had refrained from commenting or mentioning it to Catherine. She'd had enough on her plate as it was. Besides, he could be wrong, and it could be nothing. He noticed Eve's frown, so he was sure she picked up that last thought in his mind. He turned his body a little towards them, so she could see his reassuring smile. She smiled in return and turned her attention back to Sue, who had now reached her "colourful teens" stories as she referred to them.

Romy and Deborah were talking animatedly, which he thought was a good thing, as Roy was forced to turn his attention to Martin, which he thankfully did. From what Tristan could hear, Martin was into fencing, which fascinated Roy, who basically was a sucker for anything weapon related. He heard Roy taking Martin up on his offer to drop by his club for a tour and lesson. That would be right up his alley. All together this was a remarkable group of people. Catherine's friends had such a different outlook on life and how to use and handle their gifts. It had made him rethink his own course in life. He'd noticed the change in Eve immediately. She was more relaxed and certainly more outgoing than he was used to. He liked the new Eve. Though it pained him to admit it, he realised that was mostly Alan's doing. Catherine had rubbed off on him in the same way. Tristan wasn't one to doubt orders. Sure, he did things his own way, but he always delivered. At the Company, if you didn't follow orders, people ended up hurt or dead. Catherine had made him rethink the course of his life. Probably the reason why he didn't like her involvement in the Company. He was afraid it might change her. And he didn't want her to feel like she had no choice. He would make sure she had a choice.

Another tasting course was delivered and Leah led by example. She took her plate and glass and walked over to their table. Sue, Romy and Martin got up as well and moved towards the other table. He saw Alan also getting up thanking Meg and Harry for a lovely conversation before he came over to join Tristan's table. He pointed to the empty seat next to him.

"Do you mind? Alan asked.

Tristan made a waving gesture with his hand. "Be my guest."

"Hello, fellows, can I join the party?" Catherine asked, taking a seat on Alan's other side. They both smiled at her. Deborah scooted closer to Roy, who remained seated, obviously pleased she came to sit next to him. Eve got up as well, but only to take the empty seat on Tristan's left-hand side. Charles remained seated at his own table.

"That Meg is an extremely interesting woman," Alan said to both Catherine and Tristan. "And I think I got her open to the idea of exploring her powers."

Tristan couldn't help himself. To be frank, he had been wondering about Meg's abilities himself. "Really?" he asked. "Could you sense something greater?"

Alan nodded. "She certainly has the potential. I think what's holding her back the most is fear of actually hurting someone. Let's be fair. It's not a 'nice' kind of power. It used to scare the bejesus out of me."

"Why do you think she would be open to learn more, though?" Catherine asked.

"Well, I explained to her that death can also be a gift. Or an act of mercy. Think of animals hurt beyond repair. People dying of terrible cancer or other diseases. Her gift can be a force for good. After all, we all know it's all about intent."

Catherine looked a bit dumbstruck, and Tristan could feel her confusion. He was sure Alan would feel the same thing.

"You're surprised," Alan said to Catherine. "Did you ever stop to consider that I too was still discovering who I was and what I could do? Look, I know I took matters in my own hands, and I'm not saying I wouldn't in the future. However, I would like to think that I wouldn't hurt anyone out of spite. Also, I believe there has to be someone, or a group, who deals with all the bad things when our legal system fails. And it fails way too often, Kate. You know that."

Tristan sighed.

"You don't agree?" Alan asked.

"No. I sighed because I actually do agree. How could I not? I'm working for the 'group' you just described."

"Still, it's very dangerous to hold that much power. I mean, who are we to decide who's right and who's wrong?" Catherine mused.

Alan smiled.

"What?" Catherine asked.

"That's exactly why the Company needs someone like you, Kate. If there's the slightest chance someone could be innocent, you would look into it until you uncover the truth. They need someone like that. The world is changing. I think the people in charge realise they have to change as well, if they want to survive. It's a whole new world out there. It's not just good or bad people with guns anymore. It's religion, equal rights, viruses, biological warfare. The world is thrown off balance. You of all people should be able to feel that."

Tristan looked at him. "You think that's the reason they want her on board? For her vision?"

Alan nodded.

Eve, who had been listening, had a thoughtful look in her eyes. "Well, that and, of course, it would be the cherry on the cake. Just think, a true elemental. I know they're hoping I will see the light and come back. And they're betting Alan is not willing to let me go and tag along."

Alan snorted. "Well, then they would be betting on the right horse, yes."

Eve smiled at him. "Between the four of us, we'd make a pretty unbeatable team. Wouldn't you agree?"

"I see your point," Catherine said. "Frankly, I don't care what their motive is. I know Tristan is happy to be on good terms with Eve, and I'm thankful to have Alan in my life again. I am." She looked at Alan.

"I know," he replied with a smile. "Empath, remember?" He winked.

"Right. Still, sometimes it needs to be said out loud. Anyway, now we're all at this table, how are we going to go about this tomorrow? Lee, what was it exactly you said to

Charles again earlier this evening?" Catherine asked.

Leah, who had been talking to Deborah and Roy, looked around.

"Sorry, hon, could you repeat that?"

"You said something to Charles earlier this evening. Something new about your vision."

Leah nodded. "Oh, right. I saw a shooting. It ended badly. I think they have a lot of idiots, excuse me, people, on the inside who'd stop at nothing to make sure they succeed. So, I would suggest wearing a bulletproof vest. I mean, if we're going as NYPD, that wouldn't raise any suspicion, right? And Alan, Tristan, Kate and Eve are going to need all the help they can get."

"I don't think it's a good idea to have you involved on the rooftop, Leah," Tristan said. As soon as the words had left his mouth, he could feel her resistance. "I'm just saying we need you on the ground. We have to see them coming, and you are our best shot when it comes to vision."

Leah looked taken aback. "Oh. Right, hadn't thought of it that way. How will I get any information to you, though?"

"Roy can hook you up. Right, Roy? Roy?" he said, a little louder than the first time.

"Sure thing, boss. Hook up, absolutely. Uhm…who exactly?"

Tristan rolled his eyes while everybody at his table smiled. "If you could leave Deborah alone for one tiny second, you might actually be interested to hear what we're discussing. We're going over the schematics for tomorrow. Who's coming, who will be on the actual rooftop, who in the building and who's going to sit this one out?"

"I'm sure as hell tagging along," Deborah said immediately.

"Actually, I was hoping you would agree to be Leah's back up," Tristan said.

Both women looked at him.

"I'm not a seer, Tristan. You know that," Deborah said to him.

"Yes, I do, but we have to think of everything. If something happens to Leah because she has her full focus on us and she can't get the information through, we need a backup. Now, Roy can hook you up as well, but should all else fail, I'm counting on your abilities as an empath to feel a dark presence with bad intentions in time to get the two of you out of there. Do you think you can handle that?"

Deborah raised her chin and had a fierce look in her eyes. "Absofreakinlutely."

"It will be dangerous. Deborah, I mean that. Leah, that goes for you as well. This is nothing like the asteroid. With the asteroid, basically all of us were willing to die at some level. It wasn't someone out for revenge. It was just nature. These people, they will be out to stop us, at all costs, and they will stop at nothing to succeed. They will shoot first and ask questions later."

"Yes, yes, they're the cuddly type. We get it. We're not sitting this one out, Tristan, so don't even bother," said Deborah.

Leah nodded to confirm she agreed with everything Deborah had just said.

"Who's going to be on the actual rooftop, just the four of you?" Leah asked, looking at Tristan.

"I'm still not one hundred percent sure. I think we'll bring Igor, the freezer, as well. Fine, you're not sitting this one out. However, if you'll be guarding the main entrance, then both Charles and Marcus, the shape shifter, are staying with you. Leah, Deborah, is that understood?"

They both nodded.

"The four of us will do a whole building sweep, working our way up to the rooftop. From that moment, it will mostly be up to both you and Deborah to detect anything suspicious. Eve will be joining our party of five, so I would be more comfortable knowing you have a healer nearby as well. I'm hoping Sue would be up for that."

"She would be up for that," Sue replied, leaning over her chair.

He had not realised the room had gone awfully quiet. They

were all listening to him. *Fuck! How much did they hear?* Harry and Martin looked awfully relaxed, though.

"We filled them in after the first tasting, Tristan, so everybody here is up to speed," Romy said, pointing to the rest of the table. "Actually, we would like to know if there's anything we can do to help?"

Tristan looked around, his eyes landing on Roy. "Honestly, boss, we could use all the manpower we can muster. If we're going to do a building sweep, they will be expecting an entire SWAT team from the ESU."

"ESU?" Sue asked, her chair still turned towards Tristan's table.

"Emergency Service Unit," Roy responded. "We'll be posing as them. Peter is already working on getting us two Emergency Service Squads. They drive around in trucks. We'll have to get rid of them as soon as we're inside, though. Those puppies attract way too much attention. Gilly's not a fan. She's given us a two-minute time window to get the trucks out of the area and us inside."

"Okay. So, you need me downstairs to safeguard Lee and Deb and anyone else close by. What else do you need?" Sue said, her eyes on Roy.

"Well, we could really use some help with those trucks, to be honest. Romy, how powerful are your glamours?"

"Pretty damn powerful," Martin answered before Romy had a chance to reply. He looked at his wife proudly. She gave him a quick kiss.

"Thanks, sweetie. What do you need, Roy? Do you need a cloak?"

Roy shook his head. "Not exactly. I was thinking along the lines of a notice-me-not charm, if you catch my drift."

"Hmm, that's going to be tricky." She sat back and pulled the elastic band of her high ponytail tighter. With big, dark grey eyes and hair almost as white as Alan's, though Romy's was more on the platinum blonde side of the spectrum, she stood out in a crowd. Being a fitness instructor also resulted in her having a very sculpted body. "How about this? To anyone on the street the two trucks will appear to be from a catering company. Will that do?"

"Oh, that would be perfect! Wait, hang on, won't the people inside the building see the same thing then?"

"No, they won't be affected by the glamour. Believe me, I made that mistake several times. Either it works outside, to a certain extent, or it works in a room, also to a certain extent. I am confident, however, that my glamour will be effective enough for anybody in the near vicinity or just walking by."

"Excellent! Should any Aldaw members be lurking about, they won't be alarmed by a catering truck."

"The ones who are hiding inside the building, though, will see the original truck."

"I think we'll take those odds. Right, boss?" Roy asked.

Tristan nodded. "Yes, that would help a great deal, Romy. Roy, who will have her back?"

"Martin, I'm sure you can hold your own. Willing to trade in the sword for a gun, just in case?"

Martin nodded. Romy looked worried. "It's just for worst case scenario, love. Roy has got snipers on the roof, right Roy?"

"Damn straight. Romy, it's just an extra precaution. Should someone suspect what it is you can do and try to attack you, I'd like someone close by. Besides, I understand you're quite the gymnast, so they'd probably have a hard time getting to you in time anyway, but better to be safe than sorry, right?" He winked at her.

"Yes, I guess so. I'm just not very fond of guns, that is all."

"I always wanted to try my hand at shooting," Deborah said. They all looked at her. Roy's mouth actually fell open just a bit. He closed it quickly. "What? Not to shoot anyone, obviously. It's just the whole sniper thing fascinates me. I used to shoot bow and arrow back in the Netherlands and I was pretty good at it too, if I say so myself. I always wondered if I would have a knack for shooting from a great distance."

"Shame we need you downstairs, Deb. Maybe next time," Roy said, giving her a wink.

"Charles, will you be up on the roof with us?" Catherine asked.

"I'm sorry, miss. I'll be flying up and down through the building, catching as many flying bullets as I possibly can. Hopefully, there will be zero, but from what Leah has told me, she's seeing a lot of people there. We need this to end in our favour. I'm sure, though, if you don't feel safe enough, we could arrange something." Charles turned to Tristan, but Catherine intervened before he could say something.

"Oh God, Tristan, no. Don't bother on my account. Charles, it's okay, really. I was just curious where you would be. It will be a great comfort knowing you're out there protecting my friends."

He smiled at her. "With my life, you can depend on it."

"Well, that leaves us. And knowing what my wife can do, I imagine you have something special in mind for us," Harry said.

"Tristan, would you like to explain this one?" Roy asked.

"Sure. And you're right, Harry. If Meg and you agree to this, of course. Alan's focus is not on seeing death. Leah will be focusing on any threats coming from the terrorists and will be inside the building."

"You need someone with a complete overview," Meg finished his sentence. Her voice was soft and calm.

Roy nodded. "Yes, it would help us tremendously. Especially for those who will be on the rooftop. I figured as you can see death even through still pictures, you can also see it through a pair of binoculars. Would I be correct in that assumption?"

"I never tried, but I don't see why not. It's just another filter. My power has no problem with filters."

"You will be on top of another building close by, Meg. I'll show you the schematics tomorrow morning. Harry, being the only American-born here in the group, I understand you were special forces for several years?"

"Navy SEALs, yes. I served for four years."

"SIG Sauer P226 would work for you then?" Roy asked.

Harry gave him a big grin. "My kind of weapon." He looked over at Deborah. "I never knew you had an interest, Deb. I'd be more than happy to take you along to the shooting range sometime."

"I might take you up on that, Harry. Thanks."

"So, my main focus will be everybody on the rooftop then, where the actual ball is?" Meg asked.

"Yes, we'll get you up here, you see?" He showed Meg and Harry something on his phone.

"Oh, so we'll be higher up. That's good. I wouldn't like it if I can't see everyone in my line of sight all the time."

"Well, that still might be tricky, but at least you'll have a nice overview from here. No fear of heights?" he asked.

They both shook their heads.

"Well, I guess we're going on a field trip tomorrow, hon," Meg said to Harry. He put his arm around her shoulder.

"You bring the wine. I'll bring the cheese?" he asked.

"Well, bugger, if they're having cheese, is it too late to switch buildings?" Alan asked.

They all had to laugh.

"Sorry, Alan, can't let you drop the ball."

A loud moaning and groaning arose from the group.

"Jeez, Kate, that was really bad, even for you." Alan rolled his eyes at her.

Kate just shrugged. "I thought it was pretty good. Roy, Tristan, do you think we we've got things covered for now and can go back to enjoying our night out on the town?"

Tristan smiled at her. "I think we might be able to squeeze in some actual fun. Not too much, though. Remember people, we are all jet-lagged, we will wake up in the middle of the night. We do need to be rested so we're bright-eyed and bushy-tailed in the morning. With any luck, we'll be celebrating New Year's and see that ball drop as it's supposed to drop."

They all raised their glasses again.

"Hear, hear!"

Alan

December thirtieth, tomorrow *that ball will drop, no doubt about it.* Alan had been lying awake for a couple of hours, mulling over everything in his head that was said the previous night. Today would certainly define them as a group. And he would do everything in his power they would all walk away from this. He was starting to like this group of people. For one thing, he was immensely grateful to have Catherine back in his life. They had spoken quite a bit to each other last night and he was glad to discover they still shared a lot of the same ideas, the same outlook on life. Especially when it came to running the Company. He had liked her thoughts on how to recruit people and develop their talents.

"I just don't understand why my...umm...the Serpent is taking these powers for granted. I mean, I understand they have a lot of ways to recruit new people and I'm sure they will have someone like you, who can recognize someone's powers or potential, but even then, just leave it there? From what I understand, their training is primarily focused on staying in shape, learning everything there is to know about defending yourself, being stealthy, that sort of thing. What about developing your powers? Is that just a given?" Catherine had asked.

Alan had understood exactly what she meant.

"I hear you. Actually, I had a whole discussion with Eve about this. I think you're right, though. They see gifted people as exactly that. Gifted people, I don't think they've given much thought to how to enhance them. They have done research how to best restore them, when someone is injured in the line of duty, so to speak, so they must know something. I mean, just look at me. I was in a coma for years. Besides the actual use of my body, it took me little to no time to get back into shape, which is pretty remarkable, when you think about it."

That had intrigued Catherine. "That is interesting. I thought they basically didn't do anything to research someone's powers, but I see I have to adjust that opinion. Of course, they must have done loads of research on how to keep your muscles and brain working. Still, that is cause and effect. I'm definitely going to talk about the option of a training facility. Not for 'regular' use, but focused on how to enhance your powers and research."

She had looked at him in a peculiar way. "You would be really good, you know. I can honestly say you were the best teacher I ever had. I learned so much from you. You made us think outside the box, come up with new solutions and encouraged us not to shy away from pushing through a difficult argument. Alan, if I'm really going to consider this, eventually leading the Company, I mean, will you come with me? I know what you're going to say, you are actually wanted by the same Company, but honestly, we both know that's pretty much bullshit. They would probably throw a party if a master of death would join their ranks, and I'm pretty sure the big boss owes me quite a lot. I was serious when I said you and Eve would be free to go anywhere you like, without constantly looking over your shoulder. However, I would like it very much if anywhere would be by my side."

Catherine had completely taken him by surprise. He'd been flattered, of course, touched even, but he honestly couldn't come up with a solid reason why she would want him there. And he'd said as much.

"Why? Don't get me wrong, I'm flattered. Hearing those words from you is a huge ego booster. It means you trust me again, and that means a lot to me. Probably more than you realise. You have Tristan, though. And Charles, Roy, your whole circle because they would never abandon you, not to mention two other colourful people who will probably prepare you for what's to come. Why would you need me?"

"I love Tristan. Very much. And he loves me. He will always keep me safe, try to protect me. And therein lies exactly the problem. I need someone by my side who's not afraid to disagree with me, not afraid he's going to hurt my feelings and who will be able to question my motives. You've always done that. Besides, who else is going to run my new training facility?"

He'd laughed. "I don't know, Kate. You've given this a lot of thought, haven't you? Does Tristan know how you feel about this?"

She'd shaken her head. "Not in so many words, no. He suspects, though. Like you, he can sense how I feel about people, and he's not an idiot. He knows having you back in my life makes me happy. In the end, that's all that will matter to him. Tristan's main issue is me getting hurt. He would give up the Company if that's what would make me happy. Of course, I would never do that to him. He doesn't realise it, but Tristan needs the Company. Perhaps not in its current state, but that, I can change. The Serpent might come to regret leaving the Company in my hands."

"You forget the Serpent is the greatest seer mankind had ever seen. I think it's fair to say they would be one or two steps ahead of us."

"You haven't given me an answer, though. I'm not asking for a yes or no. And obviously you will want to discuss it with Eve. I'm asking you to consider it. And consider it seriously. Will you do that for me?"

He had nodded. "You have my word, Kate. I will seriously consider it. Might I also say thank you? For the vote of confidence. It means a great deal to me."

Her smile had turned sad. "I'm the one who should be asking for a vote of confidence. After what I did to you? I honestly don't know if I could be this forgiving."

"Silly girl," he had replied. "You never attacked me, Kate. It was pure self-defence. You know that and I know that. And who knows, if things had turned out differently, you might not have met Tristan, and I might not have met Eve. Have you ever considered this could actually be the better version? Of life, I mean."

"I guess we'll never know. I wasn't planning on adding parallel time travel to my list of things I'd like to do."

Alan smiled at the memory. He had been considering her offer and had discussed it with Eve the moment they had arrived back at the hotel. Eve had been surprisingly open to the idea. She always took him by surprise. He carefully brushed a strand of black hair out of her face, which had escaped her braid, not wanting to wake her. If she would have to heal or worse, revive someone today, she was going to need all the sleep she could get. They had made love in the middle of the night, when they both had woken up way too early. After a few minutes of mutual sighing and staring at the ceiling, Eve had asked if she could braid his hair and he'd braided hers in return. It had been very intimate. Alan sometimes wore his long, white hair in a low ponytail, at the nape of his neck, whenever the weather would get too hot. Mostly, he would just let it hang lose over his shoulders. He had liked braiding her hair. She had turned around when he was done and one thing had let to another.

It was nothing like he ever experienced. Back when he had been in a relationship with Catherine, he'd still been on his guard, not wanting to let anyone in that deep into his soul. As an empath, it had been easy to block her out his inner thoughts and desires. In the end, that had been exactly the thing which drove them apart. He hoped she would get to experience this feeling of true connection with Tristan. With Eve, there was nowhere to hide. Not that he wanted to, but he automatically relaxed because there was no point in trying. He did wonder whether people in the hotel would have heard them. He remembered being quite vocal at one point, claiming her as his own.

"Take me, then," she had said to him, her lilac eyes almost

purple, burning with passion. It had driven him right over the edge. They both had needed a full fifteen minutes to catch their breath afterwards. She had fallen asleep in his arms. He had tried to savour the moment for as long as he could, until he finally had succumbed to sleep as well. A shiver ran across her spine and he gently pulled the sheets a bit higher.

She stirred and turned over. Eyes still closed, she mumbled: "What time is it?"

He smiled. "A little after nine. I was going to wake you in a moment. Would you like to have breakfast in bed?"

"Yes." Her muffled reply came from under the sheets, which made him laugh.

"Coffee, I take it?"

"In an IV, if possible," she said, her head still under the sheets. "God, I feel like a train wreck. What the hell did you do to me?" she said, throwing back the covers and sitting up straight.

"Hey, don't blame me. You seduced me, remember. I was playing nice, trying to let you get some sleep."

She snorted unladylike. "You were as much awake as I was. We were not going to get some sleep anytime soon. What, you'd rather we'd tried our hands at different types of braiding?" She let one of her hands go over her head. "What kind did you do, anyway? I had no idea you could braid."

He raised an eyebrow. "Have you seen Kate's hair? Have you seen her temper when she doesn't get her way? Right. I learned how to braid really quick. And do you even have to ask? I did a Dutch braid, of course. I think it looks nicer than the French version. And your hair is nice and thick, it looks good on you, in a Tomb Raider sort of way." He kissed her lips when she was about to protest." "Shh, don't mess up my fantasy."

She rolled her eyes. "I'll be sure to bring along my Glocks next time, okay? Now get me my freaking coffee. I'm going to hit the shower."

Alan laughed at her retreating back but picked up the phone nonetheless to order them breakfast. And coffee. Lots of coffee.

* * *

"I still think we're leaving too much to chance here. I don't like it," Gilly said.

Alan sighed, trying to stay calm. Gilly had been biting their heads off for the last ten minutes or so. She obviously hated variables and wanted to fine-tune every possible scenario. He understood that's what made her an exceptional planner, but they had spent most of the day at the Company's facility in Coney Island and they were now fast approaching the end of the afternoon.

Catherine, Eve and Deborah were lying on the couch. Alan could tell they weren't even pretending to listen anymore. He was slowly warming up to Deborah after last night. He now had a better understanding of the way her mind worked, and he sensed the feeling was mutual. They would probably always get on each other's nerves. She was too dramatic for his tastes, but there was a practical side to her character which he really liked. The side of her that was now sighing, dramatically, of course, and rolling her eyes, as is she was willing Gilly to shut up and move on. Unfortunately for her, and him, it did not work. Marcus and Igor, the shape shifter and freezer, had been keeping to themselves in a corner of the office. Igor tried very hard to blend in, trying to sit comfortable in a chair that could barely support his weight, but to no avail. There was just no avoiding the man. Eve had not exaggerated, he was huge. He looked at Marcus, whom she had referred to as pretty and could see what she meant. Not that he was jealous, or anything.

Gilly was going over the schematics again with Tristan, Roy, Charles, himself and Leah, who she had been drilling every single minute to see the immediate future.

"No, Leah, you can't say I think so. You have to be sure.

Do you see someone in this corner, yes or no?" Gilly pointed to a certain point on the schematics of the building they would be entering pretty soon.

Leah was rubbing her temples.

"Gilly, perhaps we could give Leah a break for fifteen minutes or so? If she can't focus, she won't see clearly and the information is pretty much useless anyway, right?" Alan said.

Leah gave him a grateful smile.

"Oh, I suppose. We don't have fifteen minutes, though. We need every minute we can get. Fine, go get some coffee, Leah. Get your mind focused."

"Yes, ma'am," Leah mumbled and got the hell out of the room before Gilly could change her mind. Alan followed her out of the room.

"Oh, my God! I thought Kate and I were control freaks, but this is ridiculous. That woman is out there and still speeding. I don't know what you did to persuade her, at this point I really don't care, but thank you, thank you, thank you."

He smiled. "You're welcome, Lee. Actually, this was just a regular appeal to her good nature, no empath powers at all. I would have resorted to that, though, if she hadn't agreed."

"Good! For future reference, you have my permission."

He laughed. "Be careful what you wish for, Lee. You might get it."

"At this point, I honestly don't care. Coffee?" she asked, as they had reached the coffee machine in the hallway.

"Might as well. I think a Red Bull or two wouldn't go astray now either."

"Or single malt whiskey. Probably not a good idea, though." She hit the espresso button and sighed. "Alan, I know we'll be there with a lot of people and gifted people nonetheless, but I'm seriously worried about the number of assholes I'm seeing."

He nodded, meanwhile hitting the espresso button as well and changing cups. "I know. I could feel your anxiety from across the room. Tristan can feel it too, you know. He's not too happy about your anxiety. He knows you're not one to exaggerate, which means your estimation of bad guys is probably pretty accurate. We do have quite the extraordinary mix of people here, though. What is it that has you worried? I mean, what exactly?"

"The things I cannot see. Split decisions. I cannot account for those. Free will and shit, it's a bitch. Human beings as a species are unpredictable. Pun totally intended. That's what makes this so difficult. I can only see what they decided so far. Or in which direction that course will lead them. If they change tactics before they enter the building, or worse, when they're already inside the building, I'll see it, but it might be too late to get the information through to any of you."

"I understand that more than you know. That would frustrate the crap out of me as well. But Leah, if worse comes to worst, just yell out the name of the one under attack and add, look out! We'll all be on our guard. Don't forget, you also have Meg on the other building. She can lighten your load. Let her worry about potential death and keep your focus on the bad guys."

She nodded. "That's actually helpful. Thanks, Alan."

"Hey, my life might depend on it, so you're welcome," he said, giving her a slight nudge with his shoulder.

"You know, Alan. You're not so bad. If you weren't such a terrible pain in the ass, I might actually like you."

"Oh wow, praise indeed! Well, come on, seer. You're fifteen minutes are almost up."

"Yippee," she mumbled but followed him back into the hallway nonetheless.

"Ah, Leah, you're back. Good, good, how are you feeling?" Gilly gave her a piercing onceover.

"Exactly the same as fifteen minutes ago, but let's get this over with."

"Yes, let's. Please, for the love of Merlin and everything that's holy," Deborah groaned from the couch. Catherine and Eve both sat up a little straighter.

"Okay, one more time. You will all enter the building. Marcus will personify the captain of that particular unit. Leah, you're not seeing any trouble until they are actually up on the roof, correct?"

Lead nodded. "Yes, for now. Like I said, my visions will change if their decisions change."

"Understood, but for now, you're good to go until you're on the rooftop. Now, will they be in immediate danger on the rooftop or can Kate start and try to dismantle the toxin inside the ball immediately?"

"Immediately. Kate, I will keep you updated on the crystals, though I can't be sure I can get a possible explosion in time. So, you'll have to keep an eye on the ball's integrity yourself as well."

"Duly noted and will do," Catherine replied, sitting up straight now.

"Obviously I can't check for the ball, but I will be keeping my eyes focused on everyone on that rooftop. As soon as I see any changes in your life expectancy, I will let you know immediately," Meg added.

"I was just about to say that, thank you, Meg," Gilly replied. "Good, so how long do we have before all hell breaks loose, Leah?"

"Not enough. The toxin needs at least thirty minutes, I'm seeing trouble at fifteen minutes and that's best-case scenario."

"But you can't see anything right now, can you, Meg?" Gilly asked.

Meg shook her head. "No. Which would mean in this scenario we all walk away safe and sound."

"I like that scenario," Gilly said. "Let's keep it that way. Good! So, once inside Leah and Deborah will set up shop here. Charles, it's your job to keep them safe. Marcus, you make sure no one enters that building once you're in. Sue, if for whatever reason someone does get hurt, it will be your responsibility to cover the ground floor and the staircases leading up to the rooftop. I can't have Eve going back down to heal someone. Only in worst case scenario when someone dies."

Alan noticed all the non-Company people cringe at Gilly's last remark. Both Charles and Marcus nodded to confirm they heard her loud and clear.

"I'll make sure Eve won't have to come down," Sue said, a fierce look in her eyes.

"Good! Okay, moving on. Eve, Kate, Alan, Igor, moving up to the rooftop as quickly as possible. Tristan will take point. Igor, a word of caution, only when these people are in mortal danger, use your powers to slow down time. Every second you prolong, is another second Kate will have to hold her powers to decontaminate the ball."

He nodded. "Gotcha. Only when necessary."

"Romy, Martin, you'll be getting the trucks out of there as fast as you can. Obviously, you won't be doing the driving, but we need you on board to get them safely out under your glamour. Peter will be with you and each truck will have two protective details. Needless to say, the snipers on the roof will be keeping an eye on the trucks as well."

"What will we do once the trucks are safely parked? I don't think I could bear to listen to what's going down and not be able to do anything," Romy said, a quiver in her voice.

"I get that, Romy, but it's too dangerous to get you in once we close off the building. Best I can do is to have Peter escort you to Meg and Harry on the rooftop. Here." She pointed to the building where Meg would be scanning for any signs of death.

"Martin, do you mind? I would really feel better being up there with Meg and Harry." Romy said.

"Of course, sweetie. Peter, if you don't mind?"

Peter shook his head. "Not at all, consider it done. Roy, problem?"

"None whatsoever," Roy answered. "I know Harry here can

handle a gun, but you know I like it when you have my back. We need to keep this puppy safe." He patted Meg on the head, who batted his hand out of the way.

"Yes, this 'puppy' is very grateful. Now stop it."

"Well, I think that's about it. Any questions, ask them now. We're on a tight schedule here."

"Where will you be, Gilly?" Catherine asked.

Alan was glad she asked, because he had been wondering the same thing.

"I'll be running the show from here. One Times Square has a lot of cameras, fortunately. So, I'll be your eyes and ears, hopefully, in case our lovely terrorists make split decisions, as Leah describes it."

"You hacked into their system?" Alan asked.

"Of course," she answered, like it was business as usual. "I learned from the best, you know." She pointed at Roy, who gave her the thumbs up.

"Meg, Harry, are you ready? You'll be the first to leave."

Suddenly everybody was on their feet. Meg was holding Catherine in a tight bear hug.

"Can't breathe," Catherine squeaked.

"I'm sorry. You can do this, okay. It's not a bloody asteroid. It's just a stupid toxin. Should be a piece of cake for you."

"Meg, I'll be fine. Besides, like you said, a piece of cake."

Roy walked over to Meg and Harry. "You see this little dot? That's your earpiece. You don't have to yell, or anything. We'll be able to hear you just fine. Now, if you don't mind, I'd rather attach it in your ear myself. That way I'll know it's put in properly."

"Sure, Roy, do your thing." Meg pulled back her long, black hair, so Roy could easily see her ear. He was done in a few seconds.

"Oh, I don't even feel it's there," she said.

"Good. Gilly, system check okay?"

"She came through loud and clear, boss."

He attached Harry's as well as asked him to say something.

Gilly gave them the thumbs up sign and looked at her watch.

"I'm sorry to break things up, folks, but we really have to get Meg and Harry out of here right now."

Alan sighed. He could feel Catherine's emotions were starting to run high again. He could also feel Tristan's response to Catherine's increase of emotions. Of course, he would be worried about her, trying to give her as much time as possible to say goodbye to her friends, but if he was, he didn't stop Gilly. Alan checked his watch. They were right on schedule. He had to hand it to her, she was a good planner. Or pattern finder, or whatever they called her.

Meg ignored Gilly and quickly hugged Deborah, Leah, Sue, Romy and Martin.

"See you soon," she said to Romy and Martin, who nodded.

Peter went out the room with them and after a few seconds they were out of sight.

"The trucks are waiting downstairs. If you'll look here, you can see that the snipers are already in position. So far, there was nothing to give them any alarm, boss."

"That's not necessarily a good thing," Tristan said, a frown on his face.

"I agree. It stands to reason they're already inside the building. Which means they are either very well concealed or they have infiltrated the Times Square Alliance much deeper than we anticipated. Either theory, I don't like it, but we will have to deal with it."

"Confirmed," Tristan said.

Alan did his best to hide a snigger. *God, you're such a Company man.*

"Roy, you're up."

Roy started to walk through the room again, attaching in-ear pieces in everybody's ears. He made them walk over to Gilly to do a systems check. After he had attached his own in-ear piece, he looked over to Tristan.

"Boss? Your call."

"Okay people, try to speak only when necessary and not all at the same time. We will be able to hear everyone, but if we start to talk all at once, it can create a lot of static noise. So, limit yourself to what is vital. Gilly will talk us through most of the mission. We can compare notes later. Keep your eye on the ball and in this case, I do mean that literally. We go in, get the toxin out and exit the building. Plain and simple. Anything, or anyone, who gets in our way, will be out to destroy us. Don't aim to hurt. Aim to kill. I know a lot of you have never done this before, so please let us do what we do best. Alan, tonight I need that master of death side of you."

Alan nodded grimly. "I got your back."

Tristan looked at him, his eyes sincere. "I'm counting on that. Then Romy, whenever you're ready?"

Romy stretched her neck and gave him a short nod. "I'm ready."

"Okay. Let's move out, people! Gilly, keep us posted."

"I'll have the champagne ready when you guys get back," she said. They all smiled at her. Alan saw Catherine waving goodbye to Gilly, but her eyes were already focused on the screen in front of her.

Well then, showtime! And he closed the door behind him.

* * *

"Captain, are you absolutely sure about this? I don't mean to argue, sir, but I just can't imagine how they could have gotten past our security," the security guard said to Marcus.

"Believe it," Marcus grunted. "Go, go, go, people. This ain't no picnic!" He turned to the security guard. "Now, I want your people out, and I want them out now. We don't want any headlines in the papers that we shot the good guys by accident, now do we?"

"No, sir. I'm on it, sir."

"Make sure they take their belongings with them. We wouldn't want extra work, looking for bombs that aren't there."

"No, sir." He pushed a button and the alarm went off. "Please bring all your belongings with you and move in an orderly fashion to the nearest exit. This is not a drill. Refrain from running and look to your Emergency Response Officer for further instructions."

"Okay, people are moving out of their offices," Alan heard Gilly in his ear. "So far, so good, nothing strange. Crap, some people are still leaving their bags behind, we will have to check those." Alan heard her giving instructions to four of their own Company men to each location with a bag or laptop case that had been left behind.

After several minutes, he heard her again. "They're all out. At least, as far as I can see."

Marcus gave instructions to Leah, Deborah, Sue and Charles, who had disappeared out of sight.

"Okay, let's move people!" Tristan said, leading the rest of them up the staircase.

"You're clear," Gilly whispered in their ears, and Tristan opened the door. They all pushed through. Alan, who was at the far end of the line made sure the door was closed behind him. He looked up. Good God, that would surely knock the breath out of them.

"Kate, a little help here?" he hissed.

Catherine looked back down, a frown of confusion on her face. He looked up to the staircases and rolled his eyes.

"Oh, right! Sorry!" She turned around, stood still, her arms spread and immediately his whole body seemed to be floating. And then they were running up the stairs like nothing could hold them back. Alan felt a rush of excitement pumping through his veins. He could feel the others' elevation as well, some having never experienced something like this in their entire lives. A few of the Company men left them behind on several floors, probably checking the rest of the building and the left behind bags and laptop cases.

"Wow guys, you sure are a sight to be seen," Gilly said in his ear.

In no time, they had reached their destination. Tristan waited for Gilly and after a few seconds, her voice could be heard again.

"Good to go, boss."

Tristan opened the door and Alan could feel the cold coming through, even though he was still nowhere near the exit. Moving outside, he was glad his jacket was windproof.

"Kate, will the wind be a setback?" he asked.

Catherine shook her head. "No, I don't think so. It has never bothered me before. Where should I start?" she asked, looking at Tristan.

He took her by the hand, leading her to a full view of the ball.

Alan had to admit, it was rather magnificent up close. Hard to imagine the world's most poisonous substance was hiding inside it. He kept close to Catherine and Tristan, his empathic powers at the ready full force. Eve was hot on his tail. He noticed Igor kept circling around them.

Catherine made a gagging sound, which made them all jump. "I'm fine. It's just that I can feel it. God, that's really bad stuff!"

"Are you okay?" Tristan asked.

Alan rolled his eyes. She was obviously fine. *One one thousand, two one thousand, three one thousand.* He saw Eve hiding a grin.

Catherine nodded. "Yes, I'm fine. I'd better get started then, right?"

Tristan nodded. "Okay, now remember, on my mark, so Gilly can set the counter." He looked at her for confirmation and started to count. "In five, four, three, two, one, mark."

"And counting," Gilly confirmed.

Alan could feel a rise in temperature almost immediately. "Slowly, Kate, slowly. Don't let it heat up too fast. You still have plenty of minutes to go," he said to her and he could feel her adjustment in response.

"Good girl," Tristan said to her before Alan could say anything. "Eve, anything?"

Eve shook her head. "No, if they are in the building, they're not yet close enough for me to hear them."

"Meg?" he asked.

"You all still look alive and kicking," Meg came through loud and clear.

"How's the view on your end?" Alan asked.

"Petty amazing, actually. Bit cold, though. We should have brought our own elemental for some heat."

"Something's changing."

Alan froze. That was Leah's voice.

"Leah, what do you see?" Tristan asked. "Catherine, whatever you hear, you keep going, okay. You're our only shot at this."

Catherine simply nodded to convey she'd heard him.

"I'm not sure, Tristan. They've made some last-minute changes. I'm seeing a dark room. It's almost empty. Storage, maybe? They're getting something that's inside. I can't see what it is, it's too dark."

"Team one, move to storage room now," Gilly commanded.

Alan could hear feet moving through the hallways and the sound of doors opening and closing. After a few minutes, a voice replied, "Nothing, boss. Whatever was here, it's empty now. Just regular stuff, office supplies and such."

"Confirmed," Tristan said.

"We're approaching the fifteen-minute mark, people. Look alive," Gilly said.

"Tristan, Alan, back to back. You're both targets. It's swirling around you," Meg said.

"Shit!" Alan said with Tristan already jumping near him. Tristan kept his eyes on Catherine, while Alan focused on the main entrance point.

"I can hear them," Eve whispered. "Three of them."

"Three confirmed in upper staircase. Heavily armed. Please confirm," Gilly said, her voice calm.

"Three confirmed," Tristan replied.

"Eve, get out of the way," Alan growled and she moved to the other side. Igor came circling back, eyes on the door.

"Not unless absolutely necessary, Igor," Tristan hissed.

As soon as the door opened, Alan reached inside for the blackness to manifest. He let it roll into his hand. Before the first man was well and through the door, he hit the ground. Dead. The second guy jumped to the side and was already firing. Alan hardly had time to register it was an automatic, when he heard Eve's scream behind him.

"She's hit. Kate's been hit!"

Fury rushed through Alan. With one squeeze of his hand, he stopped the attacker's heart. He heard Tristan yelling instructions to Eve to heal her, meanwhile kicking the shit out of the third attacker. Tristan had managed to disarm the guy, but he was now facing a knife. Taking one look at Eve, he saw she was not using her reviving powers. Hurt then, not dead. Alan made a split decision. Tristan first. He turned around to finish off the third man, when he saw Tristan jump up in the air to grab the man from behind and heard a loud snap. He broke his neck. He could feel the hate rolling of Tristan in waves.

"Kate, are you okay?" Eve said, Tristan already by her side.

"There's movement downstairs," Gilly said, her voice duller than before. "Two people, a man and a woman. They're Caucasian, they don't look like Aldaw at all. I don't recognize them. Running a facial recognition right now."

Alan kept moving his eyes back and forth from Catherine to the door and back again.

"Ah crap, that hurt!" Catherine said, and Alan let out a sigh of relief.

"Please tell me you got him?"

Tristan nodded, a grim look on his face. "We got him, all right. Are you okay? Can you continue?"

"Pay attention, people, they're almost there!" Gilly's voice sounded more alert.

"Stand down. Stand down," Alan heard Leah say. "I'm pretty sure they're friendlies, so to speak. Yes, I think, I think it's the

Serpent. Don't ask me how I know this. You just have to trust me on this."

Catherine got up, right as the door opened. Igor tensed, ready to move into action, and Alan had his hand already in the air. It was Catherine's grandmother, all right. He recognised her from pictures Catherine had shown him in the past. He realised Leah would have jumped to the same conclusion.

"No time for pleasantries, people. Tristan, let me through," Catherine's grandmother said, William moving with her every step.

"They're coming!" Leah yelled in his ear, completely forgetting Roy's instructions. "Ten of them! At the very least, maybe twelve. I think you should get out of there!"

"She's right," Meg confirmed. "You all have it now. Get the fuck out of there!"

"Nobody's moving," William hissed. "Catherine, she will take over for you. You keep those bullets out of the way, use your powers. She can only control fire, let her do this. I will back you up. Tristan, Igor, get those bastards. Alan, kill and destroy. Eve, stay out of the way and keep yourself safe, for goodness sake. Gilly, restart the timer on my mark."

"Yes, sir."

Catherine looked at her grandmother, who briefly took her hand before turning her focus on the ball.

"In three, two, one, mark," William said.

"Countdown restarted," Gilly confirmed. "Hostiles approaching in less than ten seconds."

Alan switched places with Tristan, moving closer to Catherine. "Back to back?" he asked.

She nodded and looked him straight in the eyes.

"Remember, Kate, aim to kill, not to wound."

"Right now, not a problem," she replied, before the door opened and all hell seemed to break loose. Bullets were flying everywhere. Catherine used her power of air to let the bullets drop to the ground before they hit anything, sending a blast of lighting into one guy's chest. He was thrown back into a corner. Alan killed two in one go while Igor and Tristan were both engaged in a hand-to-hand combat.

"Five more minutes," Gilly said over the noise, and Alan took a quick look to see whether the Serpent was still holding her own. William was keeping up some sort of invisible shield, covering both Eve and the Serpent.

"Kate! A bomb, that guy has a freaking bomb. Don't kill him. Don't kill him. You'll set it off!" Leah screamed at the top of her lungs. Alan looked around, trying to locate the guy Leah was talking about. That was what they had been doing in the storage room. Apparently, they had stashed a bomb-belt as a backup plan. Self-sacrificing fuckers! God, he hated terrorists!

"I think he's coming your way right now. One more minute, people, one more minute!" Gilly said.

Catherine moved away from Alan, focusing on the door.

Alan yelled at her. "Send him flying, Kate, way up high. As high as you can go!"

Alan saw the Serpent hissing something to William, who abandoned his place away from Eve and the Serpent to shield Catherine from any flying bullets. As soon as the guy came through the door, William jumped in front of her, shielding her from the onslaught of a machine gun.

Catherine rose a few feet in the air and the soft breeze around him increased tenfold. Alan saw the guy reach for his jacket and then he was up in the air, like a rocket she sent him flying. Alan watched until he could no longer see him and then there was a small ball of fire up in the air. To the people down below on the streets, it would probably appear like fireworks.

She looked around to where her grandmother was standing and took a look at the ball.

"It's clean," Catherine said just before they could hear Gilly's voice.

"And zero."

The Serpent stopped and smiled at Catherine. "Well done, my dear."

"Did we get them all?" Alan asked.

"I think so, yes." Tristan said. "Leah?"

"I'm not sure, I think there might be one miss…"

The rest of her sentence was drowned in the noise that broke loose on the rooftop. It all happened in a matter of seconds. From behind the ball, one man with a handgun came into sight. Before Alan could get to him, he had already fired. The single bullet flew through the air. He could feel Igor using his powers, trying to stop the bullet, but he was out of range as well. The bullet only slowed down, as it slowed him down as well. He could hear Eve cry out "no," muffled and lower than her voice would normally sound, as she jumped in slow motion in front of the Serpent, who stood unprotected as William was still at their side of the rooftop. A second bullet flew through the air. The first hit Eve right in the chest. Alan knew she was wearing a vest, but he still felt like the air was punched out of his lungs. Eve was sent flying backwards. The second bullet barely missed the side of her head and reached its target. As everything seemed to speed up again, Alan crushed the man's heart, just before the Serpent's body hit the ground.

"No!" Catherine's bloodcurdling scream pierced through the sky. She ran over to her grandmother and turned her around, face up. Her face was covered in blood. Everybody rushed to her side, while Alan ran to Eve, who was still lying on the ground.

"Honey, she's not breathing," Tristan said gently to Catherine.

"I know that!" she said irritably. "Eve can fix that, can't she? Eve?" Catherine looked around until she found Alan's eyes. "What? No, no, no, not Eve as well."

Alan could feel the tears in his eyes for what he was about to say. "No, she's not dead, Kate, but she hit her head. She's bleeding badly. I can't wake her up. I'm so sorry, Kate. She can't revive her."

"Sue's coming," they heard Gilly say in a very subdued voice. And they could all hear her footsteps now, getting closer every second. She came crashing through the door, kneeling down at Eve's side, not even bothering when she scraped her own knees in the process.

"She's bleeding internally," she whispered.

Alan felt his own heart stop. *Please god, no. Don't take her away from me.*

Sue kept working while nobody dared to say anything. Catherine's tears were the only plopping noise he heard, as they kept falling to the ground each couple of seconds, while she held her grandmother in her arms.

After what seemed like forever, Sue sat up straight and turned to Alan.

"She'll live. I've stopped the bleeding." He took a deep breath and sent a rush of gratitude straight into her body. It seemed to strengthen her temporarily.

Sue turned to Catherine, tears in her eyes. "I'm so sorry, Kate. I can't wake her up. I can heal her body, but her mind has to find a way back on its own. I failed you again."

Catherine looked at her, through her tears. "No, you didn't, Sue. Tonight, you saved a life." She looked at Alan. "Maybe even more than one.

Igor touched her shoulder. "You knew her." It wasn't a question. "I am sorry for your loss."

She gave him a watery smile. "Thank you, Igor."

William kneeled at her side, tears in his eyes as well.

"I'm so sorry," Catherine said to him. "You probably wish you'd never met me."

He took her hand. "Don't you say that. Why do you think she was here tonight? She would do it all over again and you know that."

"William?"

"Yes, Kate?"

"Will you get me out of here?"

"Of course, but first, you have to let go, sweetie. Come on, get up. Let go."

"Yes, of course. I can do that. Alan, Eve is going to be all right," she said to him, smiling through her tears.

"Help is on the way," Gilly said, her voice also trembling.

Catherine kissed her grandmother's forehead and sighed. Gently, she lay down her grandmother's body. She took one last look and then, let go.

Catherine

The vision, the dream had come to an end. Aisling was no more. Catherine stared into the distance, the ball right in front of her. *At least, Leah's money had not gone to waste*, she thought, having been completely blown away by the amount Leah had spent on this Skybox.

Catherine knew Leah had never foreseen this, but she was very grateful they now had a private Skybox without any other people. She didn't think she would have been able to be here if she would have to keep up appearances. At least, here she could fall apart. Not that she was. She'd been awfully calm ever since it happened. Catherine had made her first executive decision after her grandmother's demise by telling the rest of the group the truth. William hadn't been in favour but hadn't said anything against it, either. She had made it clear that what was said in New York, would have to stay in New York, and they would have to refer to William as the Serpent from now on. Her mother, her uncle, they could never know the truth.

Catherine would join the Company, as far as her family was concerned, in her capacity as an elemental. As a favour to her, they had dropped everything against Alan and Eve and reinstated Tristan's promotion. He needed the clearance to have full access to the Serpent's quarters. In truth, Catherine would be the Company from now on. Though not by herself.

She had asked William and Alan over to Leah's place this afternoon to discuss the future of the Company. Her company. Of course, she had invited Eve and Tristan over as well. As it concerned Alan's future, Eve deserved a say as much as Tristan did. William had brought along a letter for her and some papers to sign. He had brought along someone else, who turned out to be a notary. The letter was written by her grandmother, dated only yesterday. She must have written it just before she came to join them on the rooftop. She had opened the letter with slightly trembling hands.

December 30th, New York
My dearest Catherine,

I'm so sorry. Did I know, I hear you wonder? Of course, I did. How could I not? But this is not a sad day, my darling. It is the beginning of a new era. My only regret is you not getting to know me. I can't regret not getting to know you because I have known you. I've been watching over you my entire life. William has many pictures, many memories. If anyone can shed some light on the person I have become, it will be him. I loved your grandfather very much, but as I'm sure you've realised yourself, I love William a great deal as well. He's always been there for me and I'm sure he will do everything in his power to make your life as "normal" as possible.

I know this is important to you. Let him lead you. Let him guide you. Yes, there will be decisions you have to make, but your life doesn't have to change that much, Catherine. This is entirely up to you. I'm sure by now you have already reinstated Tristan's clearance and called off the chase on Alan and Eve. Call it a vision of mine. I'm sure that someday, they will decide to rejoin you. I think that day will come very soon. The Trichakra has always been your symbol. If you look into it, you'll find the patent belongs to you, always has. I'm honoured to have such a talented and loving granddaughter.

The Company in its entirety is now yours. I've arranged everything in my will. William will help you every step of the way. I know you want different things out of life, but if you truly give it a chance, I think you will like the Company. It has brought me many things. It can for you as well. I trust you will respect my legacy, but I also hope you will make it your own. That's the beauty of being in charge all by yourself, you can do anything.

I do want to apologise again for the experience with the painting.
We've had it fixed, and you own both of them. Keep it safe, keep it
hidden. It is very valuable and people will come looking for it. Bad
people. Don't let them take it.

William will make sure they will bury me in the place your mother
and uncle intended. I look forward to talking with her when she visits
my grave. None of us are truly gone, my child. We are everywhere. You
will always hear me in the wind, in the water, the rumble in the deep
when you're lying on the grass, the sun on your face when you hold
your head up high. I will be there, whenever you need me.

In love and light and until we meet again,
Aisling O'Brien,
Your loving grandmother

Catherine had signed the papers, which officially switched the
Company's hands from her grandmother to herself. Having sole
possession, she had asked the notary to stay for another moment.
She explained she wanted to do things differently and divide the
Company into three equal shareholders. Herself, William and
Alan. With the understanding that if either of them would be
in disagreement, hers would be the swing vote. Of course, there
had been a lot of protest, mainly because everybody said it was
too soon, she was still grieving, but she had held her ground. She
would run the Company, but not by herself. She had explained
she did not want an answer straightaway, but this would be the
only way she would remain involved with the Company. She also
wanted a name change, effective immediately. From now on the
Company would be the Trichakra Enterprises Alliance Company.
Eve's breath had hitched, having heard the reasoning behind the
name in Catherine's mind.

"I'm honoured, Kate. Thank you," she had said. They had all
looked at her.

Catherine had explained the combination. "T.E.A.C. Tristan,
Eve, Alan, Catherine."

"That's beautiful, Kate," Leah had said, wiping away a tear in her eye.

The notary had left, mumbling something about having a lot to arrange to get this sorted out before the new year.

William would be their "face," the Serpent, so no apparent changes would be made for the employees with a higher clearance. People like Trevor Johnsson. William would also have to train both herself and Alan to get them up to speed. They knew little to nothing when it came down to the Company's history. Eve and Tristan would assist in explaining the Company's methods and vision.

Alan would be leading a brand-new section of the Company, the training facility. Mandatory for every new recruit, optional for every existing employee, but it would be highly recommended and would be integrated in the yearly evaluation to be cleared for duty. She wasn't sending anyone out in the field who could not perform to the best of his or her ability because they never had the means to develop their powers. She would do things differently. She would respect her grandmother's legacy, but she would make it better. More human.

She would put the normal in paranormal, the natural in supernatural. And she would work hard to achieve that. She felt amazingly calm and that without the aid of either Tristan or Alan calming her emotions. She had even said to Tristan it was time to reopen the trunk. He had entered her mind and together they had opened the trunk. It had felt good. She would try to never need it again. Knowing the option was there would have to be enough. She would be strong from now on. People depended on her. On the decisions she, William and Alan would be making.

Catherine realised she would have to give up some things. She looked at Deborah, who looked amazing tonight in a long dark red velvet dress, which clung to her body in all the right places. She was talking to Leah and Roy and keeping an eye on her every few minutes to see if she was not falling apart.

She wasn't. She would have to talk to Deborah soon, though. Catherine had decided to sign over Elements to her partner and friend. It would be up to Deborah if she wanted to run it all by herself, or if she would take on another business partner. Maybe Meg or Romy would be interested, though she doubted Meg would give up her store. However, they had worked together on several projects, why not in a more permanent capacity? Deborah would throw a fit, of course, but Catherine really thought this would be the best for both of them. She wanted to do this right and the Company would need her fulltime attention. Elements deserved that as well, and she couldn't think of more capable hands than Deborah's. Besides, she always wanted her own business. Now was her chance. Maybe she should ask Leah how best to approach the subject. Maybe she could glimpse something of the outcome. No, that would be cheating.

They would be flying back to London in a couple of days with her grandmother. She wanted to be there when she would be buried. Officially, this time. She looked down at her hands. She had killed, intentionally. Even though he was going to blow up the entire place, it still felt strange. Not wrong, necessarily, but strange nonetheless. Catherine knew that given the chance, she would have destroyed her grandmother's killer. If she had just been a few seconds faster. Aisling must have known that Eve would be knocked out, left unconscious. She had taken the bullet to her chest, thank God for those bulletproof vests, but she had hit her head, falling to the ground. Their only reviver, the only reviver. Of course, her grandmother had known. Suddenly her remark "no regrets" made a lot more sense now. She sighed and immediately felt a wave of concern. Tristan. She smiled at him and he came over to stand beside her. Without a word, he took her hand into his.

One minute to go. There was a lot of noise and the countdown began, counting down from fifty-nine seconds. Slowly the ball began its descent. Catherine looked over at Leah, giving her a soft smile. Leah returned the smile, understanding its meaning. They had changed the course of history. Again. A lot of people who meant the world harm were no longer here. They would probably never stop Aldaw, or any other organisation out to destroy their way of life, their freedom, but she could stop them one at a time. She would and she had her whole life ahead of her to do that. She squeezed Tristan's hand and he pulled her a bit closer to his body. He would there right beside her. And Alan and Eve and William. All her dear friends, who were with her right now, as the ball glittered on its way down. The final seconds were ticking away. Ten, nine, eight…almost there.

"Goodbye Nana," she whispered. "Safe travels." Tristan gave her hand a soft squeeze. She took a deep breath.

"Three. Two. One!" she shouted with her friends.

Confetti, glitter and fireworks exploded into the air, while everyone around her was yelling "happy new year." She looked at Tristan, and he looked at her. He pulled her even nearer and touched her forehead with his own.

"I love you, Catherine," he whispered to her.

She smiled and looked into his eyes. "I know. I love you too. Good thing we're together then, isn't it?"

He smiled back. "A very good thing."

"Let's go celebrate with the rest. Tomorrow we have a company to run."

He nodded. "But not tonight."

"No", she agreed. "Not tonight. Come here, make me forget," she whispered.

Tristan bend his head and looked into her eyes, filling her mind with thoughts of love and comfort, before he took possession of her mouth. Catherine sighed and closed her eyes, letting Tristan fill her mind.

The Serpent Whispers

I always knew *how my life was going to end. That is the gift and curse of being a seer. I made many mistakes in my life, some which I regret. My family was never one of those regrets. Did I ever miss my son, my daughter? Every single day, but I never regretted the choice I made. I knew from the beginning my granddaughter would be very special. The first of her kind, a true elemental. Isn't that worth a human life? I've always thought so.*

Now she will run the company. My company. Not in the way I intended. And not by herself. She has chosen two people to complete her trinity. Even I would never have guessed it would be William and Alan. I certainly did not see. Eve and Tristan will be there to assist them, just like the many other special people my granddaughter holds dear.

If I could have one wish granted, it would be the wish of time. Not to prolong my life, but to give her more time to prepare. For what's to come. Because the world is changing and she will face many battles. Unlike me, though, she will not be ruling alone and in that, I take comfort.

It is good to know, that even after all these years, it happens. We make mistakes. I make mistakes. And for that, I'm thankful. Thankful because sometimes, sometimes I get it wrong.

To the Reader

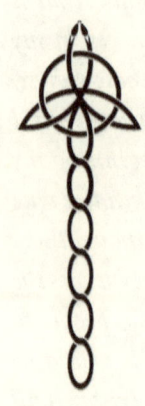

My name is Catharine van Dyk and I'm an elemental. Which means I can control earth, air, fire and water—sort of. I'm still learning and now have an entire company to help me with that. A company I inherited from my grandmother, also known as the Serpent. Only a few people were privy to her true identity. She believed anonymity was a blessing.

Me? I do things differently. The company is no longer without a name. After all, it is my symbol carved on the door, on every screen. My theory? Hide the truth well. Tell everyone. So, that's what I've been doing. By now you should know quite a lot about me and my company, Trichakra. You've been reading all about it. I know I'm not alone. There are more people like me out there. Now, it's up to you.

Look for my symbol, maybe you've already come across it, but can't exactly remember where and when. Funny how these things work, isn't it? One would almost say there's a glamour in place. Don't give up, though. Come look for me, I'll be waiting and no matter what, when life gets tough, always remember one thing…

YOU ARE NOT ALONE.

About The Author

Lisa is the author of the poetry collections *Nothing is Forgotten* and *When Words Start to Sing*, and *The Elemental*, book I of The Fire Trilogy, which was inspired by the lyrics of the British rockband Placebo. She also wrote a short story for teenagers, *The Bridge Between Yesterday and Tomorrow*, which was released late 2015. She has a background in social services and music, but writing has always been a part of her daily life. One night she dreamed the outlines of *The Elemental* and took it as a sign from the Universe to pursue a career in writing.

She grew up in a small town in the Netherlands where her parents always taught her to think outside the box. She has a degree in social studies and joined the Order of Bards, Ovates & Druids as an adult.

Lisa loves London—according to her, "the city where magic dwells"—and can often be found there. She still resides in the Netherlands, however, with her partner and their dog, Miss Ginger Rogers, and if you're lucky, you may find her in her favourite coffeehouse, Barista cafe.

Lisa is also an editor for Harp Magazine, a magazine published by The Dutch Harp society.

www.the-elemental.co.uk